The Citadel

Caleb Book 1

by MB Mooney

This is a work of fiction. Names, characters, places, and events are products of the author's imagination or are used fictitiously.

www.mbmooney.com

This book is dedicated to those fighting injustice in all its forms.

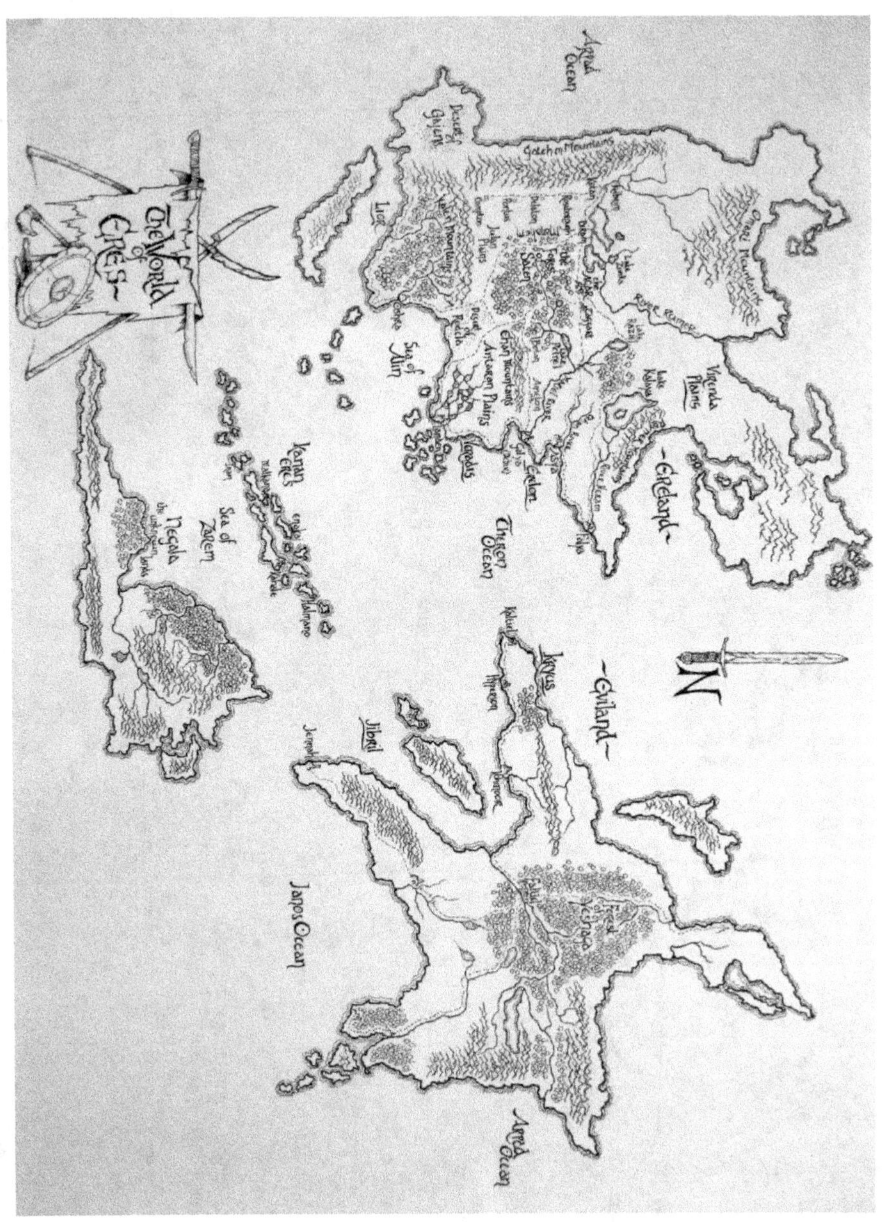

The World of Eres
Agred Ocean
Desert of Ghun
Gelchan Mountains
Lier
Sea of Jún
Tigor Ocean
Erelend
Vironda Plains
Sea of Zalem
Negola
Verlain Cliffs
Evíland
Kryas
Jíbrí
Japos Ocean
Agred Ocean
N

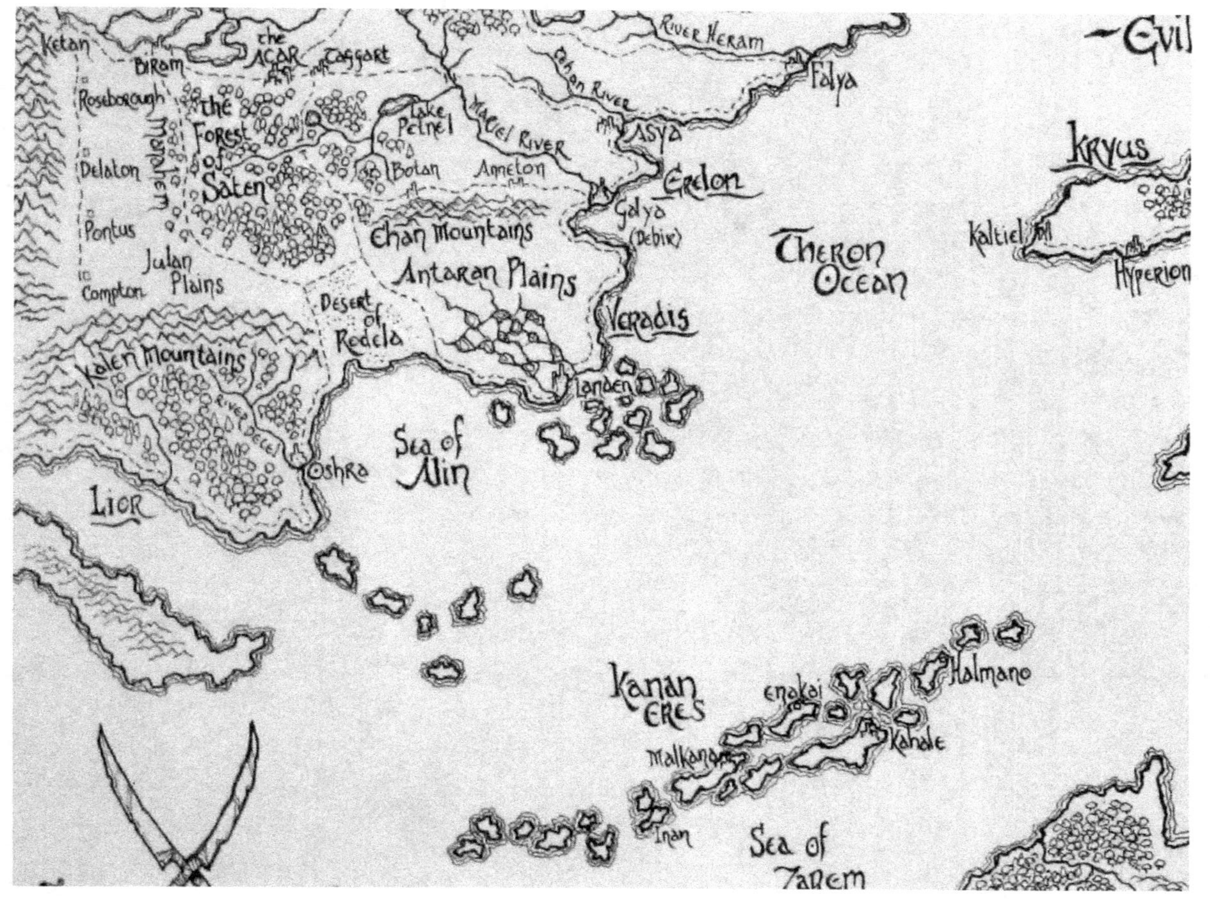
Ketan
Biram
the Acar
Caggart
River Heram
Evil
Roseborough
the Forest of Saten
Mapherm
Lake Petrel
Maciel River
Chon River
Falya
Asya
Delaton
Botan
Ameton
Erelon
Kryus
Pontus
Chan Mountains
Galya (Debix)
Theron Ocean
Kaltielm
Julan Plains
Antaran Plains
Hyperion
Compton
Desert of Redela
Veradis
Kolen Mountains
River Delel
Landen
Oshra
Sea of Alin
Lior
Kanan Eres
enakai
Halmano
Malkanar
Kahale
Inan
Sea of Zanem

Eres Chronicles:

The Living Stone

The Blades of War

The Fire Reborn

Elowen:

Shield of the King

Caleb:

The Citadel

Chapter 1

The Memory That Made Me

My time is growing short. My death looms like a dark figure breathing just behind me, over my shoulder. It is patient. It waits. I've known for years how this journey would end, and now that I can see the end of the path, I've done a great deal of thinking about the past, what it all means, and the future.

I wonder what I will leave behind. Is it common for those aware of the inevitable crunch of time to do so? If I am but a tool, a sword in the hand of El, does it matter? Am I fool to ask these questions?

Fool or not, I do. I've been called worse.

You will forgive what follows. You know me as I am but not how I came to be.

There are great battles to come, more destruction, miracle, and mystery ahead before I can rest. Perhaps you won't survive the evil days to come, and I write this for nothing.

But I don't think so. I believe you will emerge from the flames of war as exactly the person our world needs. We saw that in you at the beginning.

Others saw something similar in me, years ago, when I was only 15 years. The end is near, but I pray for the time to share what needs to be said. And by writing these stories down, I hope you'll learn from my mistakes. For I made many. I still make them.

Maybe I'm only writing for my own selfish benefit, yet I feel El wants me to put pen to parchment for you. So, despite the fact I'm not much of a storyteller, I will.

I chose this journey, as tragic as it may seem. Even if I had chosen a different path, I would have lived with the ghosts of sorrow.

Some memories require effort; I need to search to bring them forward.

Others haunt me, with me always. They are still as real and stark as the day they tore my heart in half. I can kill the largest, fiercest trodall, but I can't keep those haunting memories at bay. They are immortal. I can't win.

This is the memory that made me.

I was young, not even a decade old. My sister Carys was much younger.

Our home sat at the foot of the mountains outside the town of Anneton, a cabin made of logs and thatch with two rooms - a tiny one for my parents' bed and the large main room where Carys and I slept and meals were prepared. We gathered around the hearth, and my father told stories or read from old parchments forbidden by the elves for anyone to possess, even less to believe.

But you can't control ideas. You can't chain belief.

Da would often read one particular prophecy from the scriptures, one of a man who would rise up and lead humanity back to freedom from oppression. The prophecy of the *Brendel*, the sword of El. He would read and then stare off into an unseen distance.

A tiny path wove through a thick forest up to where our home was hidden. Father had cleared land years before, and my parents planted a vast garden full of vegetables. Beyond that, chickens clucked and squawked in a pen. Father would also hunt.

We were healthy. We were happy.

Our home had another function – humans who followed the forbidden god of El would come and stay with us. We were a haven from the elves and their soldiers, the militan.

On that day – a day without a name but real enough, and filled with enough evil that it should have one – my father was away. My mother, Carys, and I were home.

Mother cleaned freshly pulled vegetables from the garden at the wash-sink. She stiffened. Her head lifted.

"Caleb." Her voice was quiet and dangerous. Carys and I froze. Mother turned to me, her eyes narrowed. "Take Carys to the safe place. Now."

I stood from the floor, and Carys grabbed my hand, rising with me. We both knew the safe place. And why we would have to go there. I strained to catch what Mother heard but could only detect chickens and their useless wings.

Then other noises reached my ears – twigs snapping from the woods, the rustling of cloth, a clink of steel.

The elves were on the way.

Among the distant rustling, a high-pitched screech echoed through the forest.

I looked at my mother. "You're not coming?"

Mother glanced around the room then caught my stare with her own again. "They have a grider."

That screech belonged to the grider – a winged, blind animal captured from the deep caves across the ocean and trained by the elves to use its hypersensitive nostrils to hunt humans.

My mother grabbed a knife from the kitchen counter and rushed to us. She kissed our heads. "I have to draw them away from you first." She used the knife to slice across her palm, fresh blood pooling there. "Whatever happens, protect your sister. I'll be right behind you, my love. Now go!"

My feet were stuck to the wooden floor, my heart pounding. Mother took my shoulders, turned and pushed me toward the back of the house.

Then I ran.

I pulled Carys behind me. I wanted to go faster but couldn't because her little legs couldn't keep up. Carrying her would have slowed us down more.

We ran together through the trees deeper into the foothills, the ground on an incline. We passed larger boulders and less vegetation. I didn't follow a path; one didn't exist. Father had taught me to weave my way to the safe place, keeping my feet on stone as much as possible. Carys and I were panting and sweating when we reached the cave.

No one could see the small opening, hidden as it was behind other rock formations and brush. My father had chosen it well. I pulled Carys into the cave, and we walked further in, past the edge of light and into darkness. I fumbled around in the dark with one hand along the wall, the other holding my sister's hand.

There, some twenty mitres in, I found the blankets and stores of food and water. We could stay here for many ninedays.

I sat with my back against the wall, and Carys climbed into my lap. She was crying, so silent I didn't hear it before. I held her.

We waited for my mother, but part of me knew. I fought it down, dismissed it, ignored it. But that isn't how it works.

My mother didn't come. What did reach us were her screams.

The cave was far from the house. I was too young to know how far. We were close enough, however, to hear my mother wailing in pain and fear, a faint sound, barely audible, fading in and out.

Carys sobbed louder, her weeping echoing off the jagged walls of the cave.

I imagined what the elves were doing to her to cause those screams. Even at such a young age, they were not pleasant thoughts. My body jerked to get up and run to her to help her, to save her, to fight those elves.

Carys grabbed me tighter, a desperate thing, her face buried against my neck. "Cubby," she whispered her name for me like a prayer.

We were under clear and strict orders from our parents – if sent to the cave, we would stay there, no matter what happened, until someone came for us or the food and water ran out. But I wanted to run and help my mother anyway. No rule could have stopped me.

Nothing except for Carys. I couldn't leave her. I needed to stay and protect her. As much as I needed to fight for my mother, I needed to stay with Carys more.

Whatever happens, protect your sister.

I felt like a coward. Even after all these years, I still feel that shame. I know it's not true, but feelings don't care about truth sometimes.

Carys saved my life that day. I would've run to help my mother and died right along with her. My love for my sister stopped me.

I held her closer. I gritted my teeth as she wept on my shoulder.

I didn't leave, but in my heart, I made a vow, to myself, to El, to anyone and anything that would listen.

One day, I would kill as many elves as I could. I didn't know how, but I would. Or I would die trying.

My sister and I stayed in that cave for seven days before someone came. It was my Uncle Reyan, my mother's brother, also known as the Prophet, a preacher of El. He was a hard and difficult man. He wasn't much older than my da, but his skin was like leather, his face a constant scowl. His eyes, though, could penetrate any defense.

Carys ran to him. He knelt and embraced her.

I stood to my full height. "Where's Mom?"

Reyan averted his eyes for a moment, and I could have said the words before he did. "I'm sorry, Caleb. Your mother is dead."

Carys cried and fell further into his arms.

My fists clenched. "And Da?"

Reyan hesitated. "Your father is gone, too. You live with me now."

He led my crying sister from the cave. I remained for another few moments before following them.

That is how we came to live with Reyan, Aunt Kendra, and my cousin Earon. And why, when given the choice, I would become a weapon, a blade to kill any and every elf I could.

Chapter 2

Faith or Fear

"What do you mean, we're leaving?" I said.

My cousin, Earon, smirked at me. "I don't know how that's confusing. Da just told me. Pack up 'cause we're headed out tomorrow."

I sat on the edge of a cot in a back room of a shoe shop in the city of Landen. Calling it a room was generous; it was more like a closet barely big enough for me and Carys to squeeze in there to sleep.

I groaned. "But we just got here."

Earon was three years older than me and a little taller. Thin and lanky, he had dark hair and eyes. "We've been here for almost five days, Caleb. We've been other places for less."

That was true. Carys and I had lived with my Uncle Reyan, Aunt Kendra, and Earon for a little more than five years, and we never stayed anywhere more than a month. We hunkered in small apartments or storage rooms, not ventilated well or too drafty, staying with humans who would hide and protect a wandering preacher defying the Empire by daring to speak of El, the Creator.

My parents had hidden rebels like us, as this shoemaker did now.

The back rooms – closets and storage areas – were filled with stale and heavy air of the southern port city. Water surrounded Landen, and the walls didn't guard against the humidity. They only contained it.

At almost fifteen years old, this was my life.

"I don't have to like it," I said.

Earon leaned against the tattered door frame. "No one said you did."

I growled and rose from the cot. When I shouldered past Earon, he rocked back on his heels. He was taller and older, but I was stronger, the better athlete.

My cousin grunted. "Wait. Where are you going?"

Silent, I continued down the narrow passage to the larger storage room, piled with wooden crates, and most had been stacked high against the wall to give space in the middle.

Aunt Kendra knelt in a corner, beginning to pack. Kendra was also tall with longer, straight dark hair tied back, and when I entered, she stood to her full height, stretching her back. She smiled. "Hey, Caleb."

I grinned back. "Good morning." It was difficult to stay upset in her presence. She emanated love and acceptance, calmed me.

Carys sat cross-legged in another corner playing Roundback, a single player version of Tablets. My sister also glanced up for a moment but then went back to her game.

Reyan sat in the center of the room on a small barrel, and he leaned over parchments spread out across the top of a larger crate like a table. The parchments on the left were written in the First Tongue, an ancient copy of the Fyrwrit, one of the two sacred texts of El along with the Ydu.

Reyan translated the old writings into the Common Tongue, the Kryan language, on new blank parchments on his right.

Since the Kryan Empire had conquered and colonized the human lands, the elves had converted all documents and communication to their own language, over hundreds of years, until only a few rebellious humans like Reyan even knew the First Tongue, much less the older forms, and my uncle spent countless hours of his life translating sacred texts into modern common so everyone could read those parchments.

Reyan was motionless except for a slight turn of his head from the ancient, worn parchments to the newer, and the meticulous movement of the ink pen in his right hand.

After a moment, I had to collect my anger to get the courage to talk to him. "Are we leaving again?"

The room fell quiet, tense.

Reyan finished a word and paused. "I thought you would be glad to leave, the way you complain about your room."

"You mean the rat motel?" I stuck my thumb over my shoulder. "No, it's critty. But we just got here."

My uncle inhaled and sat up straight. He slowly, methodically moved his hand with the pen away from the parchments. Reyan looked up at me. "One of our contacts has been compromised. The elves may have information about our whereabouts. We must stay ahead of them."

"How do you know they've been compromised?" I said. "You have evidence he was taken or something?"

Reyan frowned. "You know better than that. *She* missed a check-in point."

"So you don't know." I put my hands on my hips.

"I know she missed the check-in," Reyan said, "and I know we must be careful."

In my periphery, Carys raised her gaze from the Tablets, and when I glanced over, she begged with her eyes to just let it go. We all knew nothing was going to change, talking with him.

"We're going to run, then, even though we don't know for sure what's going on." I shrugged my shoulders. "You're not even going to investigate and see what happened to her?"

Reyan inclined his head. "Someone will, as you know. Just not me."

"No, we scurry away like roaches when someone lights a lamp," I said. "The last thing we'll do is stay and actually help someone."

"We have encouraged men and women while here," Reyan said. "We can't control how long we stay. All we can do is use the time we have to the best of our ability."

While we were using a few different words, at its heart, this was the same argument we always had. This conversation and conflict had become a familiar dance over the past four or five months.

I knew where to go next.

"I thought *faith* was your thing," I scoffed, "but you run like a bear cub from a pack of wolves. We live in fear, not courage, not faith." I pointed down at the parchments. "The men and women in those stories, did they run at every bump in the dark? Or maybe you don't really believe them."

Aunt Kendra sighed. There was a presence behind me, and with a quick glance over my shoulder, Earon stood there. Carys lowered her eyes.

"I do believe them." Reyan set the pen down with care, a safe distance from the parchment. "You think we don't take risks? Every time we meet with others to encourage and inspire them with the truth of El, we are risking our lives. If I was living by fear, I wouldn't be here."

"In the dark, hiding behind a shoemaker," I muttered.

"Trace KaTatum also risks his life and the lives of his family to give us this space." Reyan stood, which placed his stare slightly above mine. "You would rather we stand at the street corner like a cryar? Call out the whole Empire? Challenge the Emperor himself?"

"You know that's not what I mean," I said.

"What, then?" Reyan pressed. "Getting us all killed or worse, would that prove I have faith? Would you have your sister take up bow and sword and fight the Kryan legions? Are you so ready to take up arms?"

"You said yourself," I said, "humanity chose safety instead of freedom long ago, generation after generation, until we are now slaves. Isn't standing up despite the cost the solution?"

Reyan nodded. "One day, we will take up arms, but when the time is right. When El raises up the man of war, the blade of El, we will fight and maybe lose our lives. Until then, however, we will take only the risks that are absolutely necessary to spread the message."

"That prophecy." I almost spat the words. "How do you know the time isn't now?"

"We will know," Reyan said. "Everyone will know."

I shook my head. The argument always returned to this point. The writings. The prophecies. Trust them. And just hide out until then?

Reyan took a step toward me. "Now go and gather your things. We will leave before dawn."

I took a deep breath. "I'm going out for a while, take a walk."

"That is stupid," Reyan said. "If the elves are looking for us ..."

"But you said you didn't know for sure," I said. "I'm going."

I turned to the narrow passageway that would bring me to the door to the back alley, and I left.

Within a few seconds, I burst out of the warm storage area and into the alley, which might have been cooler, but my nostrils were abused by the scents of urine, death, and decay. I inhaled again and regretted it, my stomach churning.

The morning sun threw long shadows.

The next heartbeat, Carys and Earon entered the alley. I spun away from them.

"Come on, Caleb," Earon said. "You know this is dumb."

"Don't you get tired of it," I said, "the moving, the running, the hiding?"

Earon hesitated. "Of course I do. So does he. And Ma. We all do. But it's what we are, what we do. You'd rather give in and just comply with the elves?"

I bared my teeth. "No."

"You want to give up, stop resisting?" he said.

"No, I just …" My brow creased. "I don't know."

"All right, then," Earon said. "When you come back, I'll help you pack."

I heard the door open and close again, Earon returning to the sweaty rooms.

But Carys stayed, which didn't surprise me. She hated when I fought with Reyan. Soon I felt her hand in mine, no longer the toddler she was back in the cave, but she was still a child, almost ten years old.

"I'm sorry." I glanced down. "I know it never changes anything to argue with him, but I can't help it."

Carys nodded. "I know, Cubby."

I chuckled. "You can stop calling me that, you know."

"I know." She sniffed. "Cubby."

I laughed. "Fine."

"You really going away?" Her voice was soft, a tinge of fear within it that pulled at my heart. I winced.

"Only for a couple hours. I'll find a Sand-bol match or something."

"You'll come back?"

I smirked. "Will you be here?"

She nodded.

"Then yes. I'll always come back to you, to the sure. It's you and me, kiddo."

She put an arm around my waist and pulled me close.

I embraced her and kissed the top of her head. "Be good."

I released her and went out from the alley and into the city.

As you know, I didn't come back. Not for a long, long time.

Chapter 3

The Screams That Haunt Me

Finding a Sand-bol game in Landen wasn't difficult. Walking through the dirty and dingy streets and alleys, I searched for the rare flat and open spaces of the city, most of them with a stone floor, but few were hard soil with sparse, tan grasses. I came across a lively group of teenage boys that weren't under the thrall of Sorcos, the drug the Kryans gave humans to pacify them.

Landen is situated far to the south, and the heat can be oppressive. After a few hours, I wore only my trousers, removing my boots and shirt, the pale skin of my torso slick with sweat, my hair matted flat on my scalp.

The majority of the players were local Veraden boys, the rest from Lior. I was the only one with Manahem coloring and features. They all possessed skill, which made for a challenging and physical game. Sand-bol doesn't allow direct punches or kicking of other players, but everything else is fair game.

It was what I needed, the release of energy and aggression. Having to get back to the shoemaker's to pack what few things I owned, I left after the conclusion of an afternoon match, taking more than a few bruises, scrapes, and a satisfying ache in my muscles and joints.

Pulling my shirt over my head and wiggling my feet into the boots, I stretched and wound my way through the ancient seaport city of Landen.

The sun faded into the afternoon, and a light and refreshing breeze swept through the streets, clearing away enough of the stench that I felt an uncommon moment of contentment.

Then I heard the scream.

My eyes widened and tightened. I swung my head around to the sound, a familiar sound, a sound from my memory as fresh as the day it happened.

I rounded a corner and gazed down an alley. There, just beyond the street in the shadows, two Cityguard elves were beating a woman with short sticks. The woman cowered, ducking her head down and holding a bundle in her arms. One elf stood behind her and struck down. The other stood next to her, staring and grinning, his hands on his hips, a stick in his hand. Their swords hung at their hips.

Another sound accompanied her scream, the whimper of a child. The bundle was a baby.

I froze half turned toward them, some five mitres away, and every muscle in my body tensed. My fists clenched ... and unclenched with fingers like claws ... then clenched again.

The scream wasn't my mother, and I had no idea what the woman had done. A part of my brain argued for Uncle Reyan. Was she a criminal? And even if she wasn't, it was foolish and reckless to get involved, dangerous. Cityguard beat humans all the time. Would I stop every instance? Could I even stop one?

The rest of me didn't care about logic and dismissed the thoughts. My eyes closed for a couple seconds, and I was transported back to a cave in another country.

This time, I had no one to protect. Carys and the others were safe on the other side of the city. I was alone.

The woman screamed once more. The baby cried out.

I couldn't feel my bruises anymore, no longer had any aches or pains.

Opening my eyes, I rolled my shoulders and walked slowly at an angle that would place me further out of the Cityguard view while also drawing me closer. They didn't seem to be paying attention, but even if they were, I would appear to be a young man walking past them.

I wasn't.

In a heartbeat, I changed direction and sprinted toward the elves. So concerned with the woman beneath them, the elves didn't react. Within a few paces, I leapt high, and once in the air, I lifted and led with my knees, aiming for the Cityguard behind the woman. I came at him from the side and rear, striking his head and shoulders. One knee connected full force on the elf's temple.

The other elf raised his gaze at the last tick of time, his eyes widening when I rammed into his partner, and the momentum knocked both of us into the standing elf who lost his grin. The three of us, myself and two Cityguard elves, tumbled further into the alley.

I tried to get an elbow across the second elf's face, but he dodged out of the way even as he fell. He stumbled back and scrambled to keep his feet. Hitting the wall provided him assistance.

My body continued forward, and I did my best to control the descent, tucking and rolling on the hard stone ground.

The first elf groaned and grabbed at his head, dazed.

The woman gathered up her baby and shuffled away.

Rising, desperate, I sucked in a breath and ducked the club swiped at my head. Since I was bent over already, I launched my body at him and hit his gut with my shoulder, slamming him back against the wall. The Cityguard made a whooshing noise as I drove the wind from his lungs. The short wooden pole dropped from his hand and clattered to the ground.

I pummeled his ribs with my fists. He reached down with both hands and grabbed around my stomach, lifting and tossing me further into the alley.

For a second, I was weightless. I twisted my body around to land on my side, up and on my feet right away. The first Cityguard on the ground still struggled to rise. The second one pulled his gladi, his short sword, from its sheath and stepped toward me, his face a visage of hate and anger.

When he raised his blade to strike, I rushed him and caught his sword hand with both of mine, barely holding him back. I clenched my teeth, and we spun, wrestling in the shadow. With my body tired from the day of Sand-bol, my arms quivered, so I sidestepped and let the Kryan steel blade slash to my side.

The movement surprised him, and with his head lowered and arms outstretched, I took the opportunity to elbow him in the face again, this time connecting. His head snapped back, and he retreated a step, somehow holding onto the hilt of his sword.

I felt the presence behind me and cursed myself. We had gotten turned around in our skirmish, and my back was to the first elf, who had now recovered.

Something hard slammed into the back of my head, and I wilted to my knees, dazed. Another strike came across the bridge of my nose – the same object? Different? – and the world went dark for a split second and then I was on my back, looking up into the sky through narrowing, spiraling vision.

Feet shuffled. I couldn't move.

"No," one of the elves said. "Don't kill him. Let's take him back. I'm going to have fun with this one."

When the wooden club cracked against my temple, the world went dark for much longer.

CHAPTER 4

The voice from the shadow

"Hit him again, Basilus," said Pollux, the first of two elves in the cell with me.

As I was on my elbows and knees, Bailus didn't hit me, instead rearing back his right foot and kicking me in the ribs. The breath left me in an instant, and when I coughed, I spat up blood.

Pollux laughed.

These were the two elves I had attacked in the alley a few hours before. I became aware and conscious again in the basement of the Cityguard command center on the southern side of Landen, the elven holding area before the Empire sent captives on to other prisons and slave centers, depending on the individual and crime.

Or the human was never seen again, meeting some unfortunate accident while in custody, awaiting whatever sham of a hearing was next. Which would probably be me, one who disappeared.

Pollux and Basilus had waited until I was conscious to start beating me.

"My turn," Pollux said.

"There's a spot on his face without a bruise or cut yet," Basilus responded.

Pollux rammed his fist down upon the right side of my jaw. I swung my head around with the force of the blow, trying to minimize the pain. Moaning, I fell to my side, by back to them, and one of them kicked me.

It hurt to breathe, the air coming through my lungs in a strange rattle. My eyes were closed, more by the swelling than by choice.

Basilus said, "Good play not killing this crit sucker. This has been fun."

Pollux chuckled. "One thing you can say about these humans. They might be weak in the head, but they can take some punishment."

"They take forever to kill sometimes." That came with another kick.

They had focused their abuse on my face and midsection. Pollux had managed a knee to my groin in the beginning, so I learned to keep my legs closed tight and my arms covering my head as much as possible.

Only a torch outside the tiny, stone, square cell gave any light. Everything within was shadow. It stank of crit and urine and the dead. The blood that dripped from the cuts on my face and spit from my mouth was fresh, however.

"You notice the time when we start on this one?" Pollux's kick to my back was minor.

"Nah," Basilus said. "Maybe an hour?"

"Coulda been." Pollux sniffed.

With the pain and agony over most of my body, I cursed my own stupidity. I hadn't been thinking, at least not about what could happen to me. I only wanted to save the woman, the memories of Ma in my own mind.

When I really considered it, though, I also wanted to hurt those elves. Maybe kill them. That might have been the biggest reason, being honest with myself.

And now they were playing a game to see how long it would take to kill me. Not using any weapons, only their own hands and fists. I would be another wasted life, another human killed in a dark hole of the Kryan Empire. That empire had killed a host of us in plain sight and light of day, too.

They killed us everywhere. Even in our own home.

I might be an idiot about to die, but I wouldn't die on my knees. They would know. They would remember. Even if no one else did. Carys, Aunt Kendra, Reyan, and Earon might all wonder the rest of their lives what happened to me. But these two elves would have a memory.

I could do that.

I didn't pray often, rarely on my own. Living with a prophet, that language surrounded me, but it didn't feel like my own. Like I would be pretending.

Deciding to be honest, I prayed to El. *I know I'm a moronic madder and about to die for my own stupidity. But help me stand on my feet. Help me die on my feet.*

Moving hurt. But the pain continued when I was still, so it didn't matter.

I let the agony fuel my anger, motivate me along with the memories of my parents and the knowledge of thousands or millions of other humans that have died over the last few centuries at the hands of the Empire.

Rolling over from my side, I got up to my hands and knees. After a deep, painful breath, I rose to a kneeling position.

Pollux scoffed. "What the shog is this?"

The two elves were to my left. I felt and heard more than saw them. With my hands on my right knee, I got to my feet. My legs shook, and I stood hunched for a few seconds. I forced my back straight.

"Look at this dog thumper." Basilus' voice sounded impressed.

My feet shuffled while I turned to face them. I raised my chin.

Pollux barked a laugh, and the two elves shared a smirking glance.

I hawked a ball of phlegm and blood from my lungs, gathered it in my mouth, and spat the mucus ball onto Pollux's sandaled feet.

Their smirks disappeared, replaced by scowls.

Basilus narrowed his eyes at Pollux, who responded with a two-handed sweeping gesture that implied, *you first.*

Basilus first backhanded me across the mouth, blood and spittle flying across the small cell to the stone wall. Next, he struck me in the stomach with his fist, then a second time. My knees buckled, but I forced myself to stay upright. Pollux stepped in and swung a punch up and under my chin. My head snapped back, and I took a step further away from them, my legs like thin branches about to snap during a storm.

There were three more punches, but I never saw them, my eyes closed and doing all I could to stay standing.

Eventually, I failed. My will could only take me so far. El would only help me for so long, it seemed. I collapsed to the cobblestone floor, pitching forward on my face.

Their words were distant and echoed while I lay in darkness. "I've had enough of this," Basilus said.

"Grab your blade," Pollux said. "We'll finish him."

Then came the sound of other steps scraping against the stone outside of the cell. More than one person.

"First Captain," Basilus said with a tight tone.

Pollux said nothing.

Two people waited just outside the cell. One was an elven Cityguard official. The other wore a hooded, black cloak that hid the features.

"What are you elves doing?" That was the Captain.

"We, uh, you know," Pollux cleared his throat, "we were just interrogating him."

"In case he might know where some of the rebels were," Basilus interjected.

Someone scoffed.

"Is this the one that attacked you in the street?" the Captain said.

"Yes sir."

There was a moment's hesitation. "This is an agent of the empire," the First Captain said. "And he would like to ask this child some questions, as well."

"Of course," Pollux said.

"Clean him up," the Captain said. "You will deliver him to the Imperial Agent within the hour."

"Yes sir," both Cityguard elves said in unison. They didn't sound happy about it.

Another voice spoke then, not Basilus or Pollux, and not the First Captain. His tone was calm yet carried an overwhelming sense of authority.

"He will be alive when you deliver him," the voice said. "If he is dead, you will meet the same fate."

CHAPTER 5

THE MASTER OF THE CITADEL

I was, in fact, alive when delivered to the mysterious stranger.

Basilus and Pollux carried me up a flight of stairs to another part of the complex. They watched while two older human slaves bathed me and bandaged my wounds. Another elf entered the chamber and spoke in a whisper to Pollux, who nodded.

The two Cityguard were frightened. Should I be? I was ready to face death only a few minutes before. Reyan had mentioned the elves were searching for traitors to the empire in the city. The Cityguard had that excuse ready, too.

Did they know who I was? Who I was connected to?

If they knew my relationship with the Prophet, they would seriously interrogate me. And we had all heard about the elven interrogators, the Nightguard. No one kept secrets for long.

It might have been better to die back in the cell.

Once clean and tended to, Basilus and Pollux dragged me out of the complex and placed me on a horse, draping me over the saddle like a bag of grain. They took a scarf and tied it over my eyes.

The two elves led me through the streets, the hooves clomping on the stone underneath me, and after a time they stopped and grabbed me from the back of the horse. With their hands under my arms, they carried me upright and gently for a few paces. They knocked on a wooden surface.

A door opened. "Bring him." The hooded figure from before.

The room brightened beyond my blindfold while they brought me a few mitres into a building and sat me in a chair. I leaned forward onto a table in front of me.

"He is alive," the stranger said. "Which is how you will remain. For now."

"Sir?" Basilus said. "For ... now?"

"Do you know what I am?" the stranger said.

There was an audible gulp and a gasp. One of them spoke in a breath. "Yes."

"I have already commanded your First Captain, and I repeat it to you," the stranger said. "You will tell no one of this. This is the business of the Emperor. I act for him and for him alone. If you speak of this to any soul, I will know, and I will find and kill you and whomever you told. And if they repeated the information to anyone … is this clear?"

A moment passed. "Yes, sir," Pollux said.

"When you leave this place," the stranger said, "you will forget you were ever here. You will forget this young human. You will not speak of it to each other, nor the First Captain."

A silence hung in the air until Pollux said, "We understand, sir."

"I pray to the nine gods for your sake that you do," the stranger said. "Now go."

The sandaled feet left the room. A door closed.

"You may remove the blindfold," the stranger said.

I had to force my hand to rise without trembling. I succeeded for the most part. Removing the scarf, I squinted against the sudden light, a lamp in each of the four corners of the room.

The room was a large dining area with fine dishes and goblets along the wall to my left. The opposite wall had tapestries of elves in battle, slaying humans. A hallway further into the building – a house? – was in front of me.

I sat in a padded, high back chair at the end of a long, thick table made of dark, Liorian wood. Other similar chairs were placed along the side. At the other end of the table, a figure sat. The voice had identified him as a male, but he wore a black cloak and hood. He lounged in his chair, his hands in his lap.

We were alone in the room.

A plate of breads and cheeses had been placed at my end of the table.

The stranger nodded at me. "Are you hungry?"

I was, but I didn't know if I had the energy to eat. And I didn't know if I could trust this person. Or trust myself to speak. I shook my head.

"Very well," the stranger said. "Is anything broken?"

I hadn't seen my face in a looking-glass, but I could only imagine it was covered with stitched cuts and mounds of purple bruises.

I was sure this was a Nightguard, but it seemed an odd question for an interrogator to begin with. However, my hands and feet weren't bound, so I could have escaped somewhat easily, if I could walk. Which he probably knew.

But what did I know? I had never been interrogated by a Nightguard, and no one had ever described it to me. People never lived to talk about that experience.

"Ribs, maybe." My teeth clenched.

"Ah, good," the stranger said. "That will make what follows much easier."

I squirmed in the chair.

"You must be wondering why you are here," the stranger said.

"To interrogate me, like the others said."

"Were they asking you questions or just beating you?" The stranger paused. "And you can tell the truth. It won't get them in trouble."

Yeah, but would I get in trouble? "They weren't asking me questions."

"No, they weren't. You are a hot-headed young boy on the streets of the city who decided to attack the authorities. You're no one, correct?"

I swallowed. "Correct."

"Unless you're not. Unless you are someone that I *should* interrogate. Do you have information I want? Are you important? Or do you know someone important?"

I sat very still. Carys. Kendra. Earon. Reyan. The Prophet. The elf's eyes were in shadow, but I met that darkness with my gaze. "No."

"I thought not. No, if you were someone important, you'd be of no use to me; at least, not for what I intend to discuss with you."

I raised an eyebrow, which was a mistake. That hurt.

"First, some introductions are in order," the stranger said. "What is your name?"

Should I give him my real name? A fake one? Did it matter? "Caleb."

"Caleb," he said. "A fine name."

"And you?" I said. "What should I call you?"

The stranger lowered the hood over his head, revealing a Kryan elf with long, white hair, a sign he was in a latter age. His face also possessed a few wrinkles around the eyes and mouth. His eyes were a stark green.

He rolled up the sleeve of his cloak to reveal the inside of his left forearm. A tattoo of a tree growing from a stone.

I cursed, and my breath caught.

The stranger inclined his head. "My name is Galen. I am a Bladeguard and Master of the Citadel."

CHAPTER 6

GALEN

A Bladeguard? *Break me.*

The Bladeguard were the personal agents of the Emperor, superior warriors, best known as swordmasters, but also trained in strategy and other disciplines. They answered only to the Emperor and could take command in his name in any situation they saw fit. The Bladeguard trained at the Citadel.

The Master of the Citadel, then, was the master of these Imperial Agents.

While the Empire had a senate and governors, in effect – and in every way that mattered – Galen was second in command of the whole breakin' Kryan Empire.

The Kryan officials spoke of the Emperor like a god on earth, a majestic deliverer. The Bladeguard were regarded as an extension of his power, so they were also considered elves of supernatural ability.

No wonder those Cityguard were scared critless.

If this was a Bladeguard, was it possible he didn't know who I was? Maybe not as supernatural as the cryars reported.

Galen continued. "I have an offer for you."

"An offer?"

"Yes." Galen sighed. He gestured at the tapestries. "Your history. Our history. The Empire came and rescued humanity from their own violence and division, united you under the power of Kryus and the Emperor Tanicus."

It was like he quoted from a book. I didn't answer.

"It was a bloody affair," Galen said. "Many lives lost, both human and elven. The Kryan legions are efficient and undefeated on the field, but they destroyed everything in their path, such a waste. We are in dire need of a different instrument."

Galen met my eyes. "While the Empire has brought unity and safety to your people and these human nations, at great cost to ourselves, there are still many who would break from our rule of these lands. Yet they hide. They are like snakes in the grass." Galen took a breath. "You could be that instrument."

My brow furrowed. "Me?"

"You are the one that attacked those Cityguard, yes?"

I nodded.

"Exactly. You were able to strike them, more than once. That is not easy for one of your age." Galen frowned. "And you have a good form, strong yet lithe."

He spoke like I was a slave at an auction.

"How old are you?" Galen said. "I assume still an adolescent? You appear so."

"I'll be fifteen soon."

"Good. I was correct." Galen sat up. "It is difficult for us to gauge the human number of years. As I'm sure you know, the elven adolescence lasts much longer, since we live much longer. Do you read? I mean, are you able to read? I know the Empire schools aren't the best, but ..."

I sniffed. "I can read."

"Have you read the general pamphlets or can you read longer works, scrolls, books?"

My eyes narrowed. "I've read a book or two."

"Excellent. Also, when I entered the lower jail of the center, they were beating you. And yet, you weren't weeping, crying. Did you feel the pain?"

"Yes."

"Are you in a great deal of agony now?"

My jaw clenched. "Enough."

"Good." Galen leaned forward. "This means you also have a high tolerance for pain. You will need that if we continue."

"Continue for what?"

"As I said, I have an offer for you. An amazing opportunity. I wish to train a human as a Bladeguard."

My eyes widened, and I scoffed. A human? In one of the most powerful positions in the Empire? The elves only allowed humans as servants or slaves near the elves, never in leadership.

"Your reaction is valid, since that would seem an impossibility to many," Galen said. "Follow my logic, if you would. The enemies of the Empire hide, and when they hide among humans, well, it becomes quite a task to root them out. Again, we could kill all rebellion by decimating cities and towns, but that would defeat the purpose of bringing the wonders of the Empire to humanity. No, we require a more surgical solution."

I thought of several cities and towns that had been decimated by the Empire, Asya being one of them, but decided not to mention those.

"Humans are the obvious answer," Galen continued. "Now, we've employed fear and bribes, the usual, but there are … pockets of resistance all throughout these human colonies. What we need is something that no one would ever expect, a creative solution, and yet the most effective. A human loyal to the Empire could infiltrate these regions, find traitors and rebels, and take appropriate measures. This is more than a bribe or manipulation. This would take a highly trained individual capable of excellent strategy."

My mouth grew dry. I licked my painful lips. "A Bladeguard."

"Precisely."

"So let me understand." I drew the words out carefully. "You want me to be that human Bladeguard?"

"I'm offering you the *opportunity*," Caleb said. "There will be testing and decisions to make in the future. This is but the first choice. Others follow."

"But … I attacked Cityguard," I said. "Why would you want me?"

"Seems like a foolish decision, I'm aware," Galen said. "Your life was already forfeit. Those Cityguard would have killed you eventually. I have nothing to lose to give you this offer. Furthermore, my hope is that once you learn and see more of the great Kryan civilization, we will earn your loyalty, perhaps even your love."

Not much of a breakin' chance there. "What if I say no?"

"Good question. If you reject this offer, then there are options. I could give you back to the Cityguard to finish the job they so desperately desired to complete. I could kill you here and now, especially if you tried to run. Or I could have you sent away to a Liorian mine, assigned to hard labor where you would last a few days before expiring."

I grunted. "So, *death* is the other option."

"That was the destiny I interrupted, so yes, that is where you would return." Galen grinned. "And there is one more condition before you make your decision."

"Okay."

"I don't know anything of your family or if you have any still alive," Galen said. "But you will never see them again. You won't be allowed to say goodbye. No matter what you choose, you'll have no contact. Any who know you must believe you are dead, gone. It should not be difficult for them to believe. I'm sure humans are killed or disappear often."

The way he sat quietly after that statement, he was more than sure. Being a Bladeguard, breakit, being the leader of them, he was responsible for the deaths of many.

It might sound strange to you now, but even though I grew up among people of faith, people who believed in a god enough to run and hide and risk their lives, even though my parents had been genuine believers, I had not been much for religion. I didn't deny that El existed or that it was true, on some level. Faith in El had never been a priority for me. My focus and life had centered around family, primarily Carys. Belief came more to the forefront in that moment with Galen.

He had asked me to choose, which was challenging. First, no matter what I chose, I would never see Carys again. That reality settled upon me like a great weight on my heart, although I took some comfort in knowing she would still be safe.

Galen didn't move for a while, as if he understood the importance of the moment. As a being that had lived thousands of years, he probably had experience waiting.

Second, despite my ambivalence toward faith, Galen was death incarnate, sitting at the other end of the table. An elf of intelligence and skill, he was evil and responsible for the oppression of my people. With his age, he had been there at the beginning of the wars that conquered humanity, and considering his position, he had been more than a participant but a designer of it. Along with the Emperor.

Whom he had direct access to.

My father used to read to us from the scriptures of El, the *Brendel* being his favorite, the blade of El, the one Reyan was waiting for.

Which I thought was bosaur crit. Why would we wait for some man? We could fight now, change things now.

Yet here I was with death himself offering to train me to learn his methods and strategies and become an expert in the sword. I would know all the plans and secrets of the enemy. What would I become? Not their tool.

I would be their worst nightmare.

Beyond prophecy and probability, I had made a vow to myself and to El in a cave while I held my sister and my mother screamed in the distance. A vow to seek revenge and kill every elf I could.

And here, they were going to train me to do it.

I couldn't deny the divine answer to that vow.

What would it cost me? My life, which I would lose anyway.

I took a deep breath through my nostrils, my ribs protesting. I glanced at the tattoo of the tree growing from the stone on his forearm.

"Yes," I said. "I will become a Bladeguard."

Galen grinned. "We shall see. There is far to go before that happens, much more. But you have taken the first step." He waved at the food in front of me. "I would eat if I were you. You'll need your strength. We begin tomorrow."

CHAPTER 7

THE TESTING

After eating that night, he locked me in an upstairs room with a fine bed and other furnishings. An array of salves had been placed on a table next to a washbasin. Without directions, I had to do some experimentation on the cuts and bruises on my face, arms, back, and torso. The pain subsided and I slept well.

I awoke with the sun through the barred window. I rose and washed, dressed in the simple breeches and tunic laid out for me. Were there servants or anyone else in the house? Surely Galen hadn't set all these out, but I never saw another soul.

The locks of the door rattled, and the door opened. Galen stood in a fine but simple tan robe sinched at the waist with a leather belt, sandals on his feet. His white hair lay straight down his back.

Galen measured me. "Good. You are ready."

I faced him.

"The swelling has gone down." He pointed at my face.

"Those salves helped."

"Get used to them." He stepped back out of the doorway. "Come. It is time to begin."

I rolled my shoulders and walked toward him. He seemed to glide when he turned and moved down the hallway.

He led me up a back stair that wound to a door, which opened to the roof. The top of the house extended out flat in a rectangle, as large as a Sand-bol field, with a waist high parapet on the outside.

Large stones had been piled a few mitres away. Galen strode to stand next to them. He pointed over to another area on the roof where a circle had been drawn. He waved at the stones. "Move them."

I nodded and began. The first stone was heavier than I expected, and my ribs roared at me. I thought about those salves down in the room. But I moved the first stone across the roof and set it in the circle.

I heaved a breath. Fifteen more stones. After two more, sweat began on my brown and body. By the time I had moved eleven total, my clothes were wet through with perspiration and my ribs sent sharp torment through my chest. I bent over with my hands on my knees, panting, exhausted. My arms and legs quivered.

"The training will take you beyond what you believe possible," Galen said. "What you believe impossible will be proven false. That is the only way forward." He inclined his head. "You have five more."

It took all my strength and another hour to move four of them. I collapsed on my knees, heaving big, tortuous breaths.

Galen waited a minute or so before speaking. "You may quit if you like."

I wiped the sweat from my forehead. "I can?"

"Of course. At any time."

"And you will let me go home?" I said.

"No, the original options still remain. There is only forward in this life. No going back. To retreat is death. That is a truth as sure as a mountain."

Continue or die. Got it.

I raised my head and narrowed my eyes at him. Gritting my teeth, I stood. And promptly fell again to one knee. Bile came up in my throat for a moment, and I swallowed down a mouthful of vomit, leaving an acidic taste on my tongue.

Blowing a breath, I forced myself to stand. I waddled over to the stone and crouched over it. I hovered there, hesitating, then reached down and lifted the stone with my hands, raw from the work already. The pain attempted to overwhelm me. At first, I ignored it. Then I let the pain make me angry.

Something in my right arm strained, but I continued one step at a time to the other pile. With a last effort, I threw the stone over. It made a smacking sound when it hit the edge but landed within the drawn circle.

I crumpled on the roof, resting in a sitting position, my head down.

"Well done." Galen's voice was off to my right. I couldn't lift my head. "Go down to your room, change, clean up, eat, and rest. I will come for you early this afternoon."

Galen left the roof and descended into the building.

I closed my eyes and allowed time to pass, wondering if I would ever have the energy to move. Eventually, the motivation of food and the salves roused me from my position. I stumbled down to the room.

Clean clothes had been laid upon the bed. Fresh salves and a plate of food along with a pitcher of drinking water sat on the table along the wall. I stripped bare, applied the salves generously, pushed the clothes off the bed, and lay face down upon the blankets.

I awoke to knocking at the door. A moment passed before I remembered where I was, even who I was. A human Bladeguard? Train or die ...

Still naked, I rolled off the bed, my body stiff, like trying to bend thick branches of a tree. I pulled on the new clothes and started drinking straight from the pitcher.

The door swung open, revealing Galen. "It is time."

I set the pitcher down and caught my breath. "Okay." I grabbed a half loaf of bread. "Let's go."

He led me back up to the roof. A wooden pole had been stretched across two large barrels, fastened with thick rope on either end.

Galen pointed over to the setup. "Climb up and balance on the pole, in the center."

I raised a brow at him, but I took one last bite of the loaf and walked forward. The pole was chest high. Before continuing, I started to stretch my chest, my arms, my legs. Playing Sand-bol enough, I knew some basic exercises to get more limber. It helped, but not enough. My body was stiff, sore, painful, and exhausted. I assumed that was the point.

With a leap, I hit the pole waist high, gripping with my hands and swinging a leg over until I straddled the beam. My muscles tensed while I stood upon the pole, which wasn't wide enough for my whole foot but not as thin as it could have been.

My legs were wide, and my arms stuck out like wings, trying to stay balanced, my vision focused on the beam at my feet.

"Ready?" Galen said.

I risked lifting my eyes. "Ready for wha ...?"

Then a metal ball hit my forehead.

I cursed, my head snapping back, my arms flapping to no avail. I fell from the pole to the hard roof. I looked up at Galen. "What was that?"

Galen raised up a small iron orb, fitting between his thumb and forefinger.

I rubbed my forehead. "That breakin' hurt."

Galen grinned. "Block it next time."

"You could have warned me." I rose from the roof and climbed back on the beam.

"That is not how life works," Galen said.

While I got my balance, I kept him in my periphery. I wasn't fully standing before his wrist snapped and an iron ball whipped toward my face. My hand flew in front of me, and I slapped the orb away. I would have been satisfied with myself, but the sudden movement of my arm threw me off balance. I wavered for a few seconds before another iron orb struck my left shoulder and I went down again.

Next time, once on the beam, I blocked the iron orb while climbing and another while standing, all without falling.

I smirked at him.

"Very well," Galen said.

Suddenly, both of his hands went to work, pulling iron balls from the pockets of his tan robe, and hurled five at me, one right after another. How many of those did he have? I crouched, my stance wide.

And I blocked all five.

My smirk blossomed to a smile.

Galen frowned. The hands flashed, and more came at me, sometimes two at a time, all in a barrage beyond my ability to defend. I blocked another six before one hit me in the stomach and another on the cheek and a third on my knee.

The horizon flipped while I fell and landed on my side.

"Break me," I said, looking up.

Now Galen smiled.

CHAPTER 8

ANCIENT ELVEN WORDS

That evening, at dinner, Galen set a thick book in front of me next to a plate of pork jerky, fresh fruit, and bread. He had been with me most of the day. Someone else had to have prepared this, along with bringing clothes and salves to my room, but I never saw any hint of anyone else.

While the salves helped, I now possessed knots on several areas of my body, more than a couple on my face.

I gazed down at the book. *The Elements of Righteous Monarcy* by Contigus. An elven tome of some sort.

"Do you know this?" he asked.

I shook my head, taking a bite of jerky.

"Contigus was the First Administrator of King Natalus, thousands of years ago," he said. "In those days, First Administrators were more than simple administrators. Apart from the King and Queen, they were the most important and powerful elves in the Kryan Kingdom. He was wise and educated, beyond most elves in our history."

I chewed a bite and swallowed. "So this was before Tanicus, before the Empire."

"Yes," Galen said. "Much before. Natalus was a good king, not corrupt like the latter monarchs. Contigus wrote this as a series of articles on different topics, gathering the greatest wisdom of the world in his day. This, then, has become a standard and classic for our people, for any people, truly."

I frowned.

Galen opened the book and turned to page 354. The title on the top of the page – *Power and Compassion.*

"Read this while you eat," Galen said.

I did. The words of common were older and more sophisticated than I was used to, but I could understand most meaning by context if I had to move past a certain term unfamiliar to me.

We finished the meal, Galen barely eating while I consumed the large plate of food like a bosaur after being driven over the Liorian mountains.

I looked up from the article.

Galen waved over at me. "Explain to me Contigus' argument for the balance between Power and Compassion for the monarch."

"Well, as far as I understand, Contigus argues that the monarch holds power for the express purpose of showing compassion, of helping those in need, protecting the innocent. Never to further the power of the monarchy, whether by conquest or any power over others."

Galen's gaze turned distant. "Continue."

I cocked my head. "In fact, he seems to think that freedom of the individual must be the default. If the monarch must have a flaw, it is to give the citizenry too much freedom. And power for violence must be a last resort, reserved for a select, evil few, and still never without regard for the possibility of redemption. Otherwise, the monarch designed to be the hero becomes the evil he seeks to fight." I cleared my throat. "That is what *he* says, as far as I can tell."

The ancient elf nodded. "Well done. You have summarized Contigus' argument succinctly. You are sure you haven't read that before?"

I shook my head. "Never even heard of this book." Which was true.

"Impressive," Galen said. "Now, what do you think of the argument?"

Swallowing, I said, "Um, what do you mean?"

"Simple question. You've read the argument. Do you agree or disagree?"

I didn't move during a hesitation. "I guess it depends on how you define evil."

Galen's brow creased. "In what way?"

"If you define evil, as Contigus does, as any breaking of the rights of the individual, then I would agree."

"You have avoided answering the question. I know what I think. I'm asking about you, personally, do you agree with the argument?"

Was this a trap? It seemed like one, for the sure, if I was dumb enough to walk into it.

"Yes," I said. "I think I would like to live under a king like that."

"Interesting," Galen said. "Do you believe Tanicus is this kind of monarch?"

I was, actually, dumb enough. There it was. The trap.

"He's not a monarch," I said. "He's an emperor. That is a different system."

Galen scowled. "Don't argue semantics. That obscures any real communication or genuine exchange. Answer what I'm asking, not what you think I want to hear. You believe you'll be in trouble if you answer your true feelings, but that is a misunderstanding. Whether you know it or not, you are already in a world of trouble. That is beyond your reckoning, or even mine at this point."

He leaned forward. "Tell me. Be honest. You attacked Cityguard yesterday. Do you believe your answer would surprise me?"

My jaw clenched. I squirmed in my seat. I settled and took a breath. "No, I don't believe he is."

Galen nodded. "How would you say he is different from what Contigus argues?"

"The Emperor has conquered far beyond his need," I said, "into a nation that isn't his own, all based on the idea that he has come to rescue us from ourselves. And yet he fills prisons with humanity, building more to fill those, and kills twice as many as he puts in jail or slavery. That doesn't seem like he's rescuing us."

He's become the villain he seeks to fight, I wanted to say. It hung in the air, implied enough to warrant my death.

"What about you?" I said.

"Me?"

"Yeah." It was my turn to lean forward, my elbows on the table. "How would you compare the rule of Tanicus with this classic book by the wise Contigus?"

Galen's nostrils flared, and he sat silent.

I didn't think he would answer, but then he spoke. "It is often difficult to see the benefit and salvation amongst such violence as you describe. If we define the corruption within a society as a cancer, and that cancer has spread throughout the body, how much must a surgeon remove? Only a fraction? Wouldn't that allow the cancer to continue? Should we allow cancer to exist out of some notion of individual freedom? Wouldn't it be compassion to use the power of the surgeon to get every last hint of cancer, as much as he or she could find? That is a violent and bloody option, and yet it would be kindness to remove it.

"Contigus was an idealist, and he could not have imagined the corruption that would one day mark the Kryan monarchy, and the extreme measures that had to be taken by Tanicus to overthrow that mockery of a government. Had he lived in a different time, would he have amended his argument? Would he have supported Tanicus?" Galen waved a hand over the table. "We shall never know. That is my answer, however."

My mouth became a line, holding in the many responses I wished to make. I had incriminated myself enough.

Galen smiled, but it didn't reach his green eyes. "Either way, we shall have a long day tomorrow. It is time for you to get some sleep."

I sat up. "What's happening tomorrow?"

"You have passed this part of the test," Galen said. "We sail for Kryus in the morning."

CHAPTER 9

UNDER THREE MOONS

Leaving for Kryus. We would be getting on a boat in the morning and sailing for several days across the ocean to the land of the enemy.

I lay on the comfortable bed that night, peering up at the dark ceiling above me. My exhausted and drained body ached and begged for sleep, but slumber eluded me.

Once gone, I wouldn't see Carys. Not Kendra, Earon, or Reyan. But Carys was key in my thoughts. Could I leave without seeing her again? Ever?

At the same time, Galen played some hand of Tablets with me. He had been playing these games thousands of years before I was born, and there was no doubt in my mind he operated at some level far above mine. Even still, a dog could smell a trap, and I was smarter than a dog. Maybe.

A Bladeguard was meant to be completely loyal to the Emperor, yet Galen chose a human, who the elves treated as little better than animals, and one who had just attacked a couple Cityguard. And then he got me to admit I didn't think Tanicus was a very compassionate ruler, admittedly not a stretch considering my violence against the Empire the day before.

Did I really need to go down this pit and risk my whole life to be trained to kill elves? There had to be another way, one where I didn't have to sail across the world to Kryus. And never see my sister again.

Galen had threatened my death as the only other option. But how sure was that? Galen's ignorance of my connection to one of the most wanted men in the Empire, the Prophet, proved a vulnerable point in the Bladeguard armor.

Or he did know. Which really scared the crit out of me.

I had to get out of there.

I rose from the bed, tired but suddenly focused, and dressed in tunic, breeches, and boots. I went to the window. I was on the third floor, and bars covered the glass outside. I opened the window and tested the iron bars. They didn't move a milimitre when I shook them, bolted to the wood and stone on the outside of the building. If I had hours or days, I might be able to wiggle one loose over time and squeeze out, but I didn't have that time.

I went to the door to the room. Galen had locked it from the outside the night before. I had picked a couple older locks in my childhood, mostly to get into a storehouse and steal some food, all while Carys stood behind me and begged me to stop. I would have to get creative to try and get to the lock out in the hall.

When I turned the knob and pushed against the door, however, it opened and swayed out into the hallway.

I gasped. I peeked out into the hallway with bulging eyes. A dark and empty hallway. He left the door open? An accident or on purpose? If it was an accident, then El was real after all. If on purpose ... Galen was leaving me another trap.

Trap or not, I had to make a choice. No way I would stay in that room when the door was open. I would take my chances with freedom, out and on the run.

I snuck into the hallway, careful with my boots on the hardwood floors. Making my way to the stairs, I went down to the bottom floor. Probably shouldn't go out the front. Too obvious. I went through the dining hall, one lamp burning low and giving minimal light, and crept through the kitchen. My eyes had adjusted well enough that I didn't knock over any pots or pans. I took a risk through a side passage, and a miracle, it led to another hallway with a door. Moonlight lay beyond.

Scanning around me and frozen, my ears strained for any hint of sound. No movement. No noise but my own heartbeat. I walked on the balls of my feet to the door. It was locked but from the inside, so I very slowly turned the latch with immense care.

The door opened, and I stepped outside into an alley. The three moons of Eres shone their different colors in the night sky. The Landen night air was cool. Buildings towered on both sides of me. Which way to go? Left or right? I decided to go right, away from the front of the building, further into the alleys. There might be more places to hide.

As I took a step that way, a voice spoke to me. A female voice.

"Take care, young man."

I tensed and stopped in mid motion, every sense heightened. My jaw dropped, and my head turned toward the voice.

A figure stood in the doorway, only a shadow. My fists clenched at my side.

"I won't hurt or stop you, Caleb," she said. "I only come to warn you."

I straightened and turned to face her, squinting. "Who are you?"

The figure stepped into the moonlight. She was human, older than Aunt Kendra by a decade or so, with streaks of gray in her dark hair and crinkles in her darker skin at the eyes and mouth. "My name is Lyne."

"Well met. I assume you're the one that's been bringing clothes and everything."

She gave a slight bow.

I nodded up at the building behind her. "Are there more? Servants?"

"Only me. And I am not a servant, exactly."

My mouth became a line. "A slave."

"Yes," she said. "Galen is my master."

"Did you leave the door open for me to escape?" I said.

She shook her head.

"Got it." I crossed my arms. "You said 'to warn me.' What does that mean?"

"I understand why you would want to leave," Lyne said. "I know something of Galen's plan, for you to be a Bladeguard. But I would suggest that you take care. Great care."

My eyes narrowed. "How so?"

"Galen didn't leave the door unlocked by accident," she said. "This is another test."

Cursing, I put my hands on my hips. "To see what I would do?"

Lyne inclined her head. "He likely knows what you would do. Is counting on it, in fact."

"He wants me to leave?"

Lyne frowned. "Not exactly. But that is not my warning."

"It's not?"

"I am his slave, serving here," she said, "but Galen has other agents in the city. If this is his test, he has elves to find you, follow you. Do you have people you love?"

My face went blank. "I do."

"Then stay far away from them. He will find you. And those you love will also pay the price."

I scowled. "How do you know?"

Even in the moonlight, I noted the sudden sadness in her dark eyes. "I know."

I sighed and turned to gaze down the alley.

If I left, then I wouldn't be able to visit Carys, probably ever, no matter how long I eluded Galen or his agents, whoever they were. I would be placing her in danger and the rest along with her.

I turned back to Lyne. "What about you?"

"Me?"

"Yeah. Did he send you to talk to me? Is that part of the test?"

She shook her head. "He didn't send me."

"But he probably knows, right?"

Lyne shrugged. "Safe to assume, yes."

I shook my head. "Well, Lyne, looks like I'm as much a slave as you, now."

Her smile was sad. "Possibly more."

"Break me." I went back into the building. She followed me and closed the door behind us.

Chapter 10

Sailing with the Enemy

"Wait until I command you to stop." Galen reclined on a large pillow on the deck of the ship. "Remember, don't ignore the pain. Pain won't be ignored. Befriend it. That is the only way to defeat pain. Make it your friend."

Day seven of our voyage across the Theron Ocean. I was doing a handstand on the deck of the boat, part of the morning routine. A handstand is difficult, made more so by a shifting and lurching deck beneath you. The first day I couldn't stay on my hands more than a few heartbeats. Each day I was able to extend my time.

The Last Sentinel wasn't a massive ship but big enough for a series of cabins beneath and a tiny galley. The crew consisted of two elves, one a captain of sorts and the other an elf of many jobs and talents. Lyne sailed with us, cooking most of the meals and providing whatever assistance Galen or I needed.

My arms roared with agony. I wore only my breeches in the warm sun which rose in front of us to the east. Sweat dripped off my body and splattered the deck, mixing with the salt water, making the surface slick and more difficult to stay upright.

But I was doing it.

Over the past few days, Galen continued to push me. There wasn't room on the deck to run a marathon, but he directed me with other types of calisthenics and exercises to tear down every muscle in my body, many I never knew I had.

Befriend the pain. That wasn't the first time he'd said that phrase. I tried, but befriending pain was more difficult than the exercise itself. Maybe that was the point.

The deck beneath me swayed, and my right elbow buckled. My legs swung back and forth, and I stayed up for another moment before my left arm seized and failed. I landed on the wooden floor with a modicum of control.

"Ah, I didn't say you could stop." Galen sat up.

Panting, I wiped my face and rose, as well, looking at him. "I went longer than yesterday."

"The instruction wasn't to last longer than yesterday but to stay upright until I commanded you to stop."

I lowered my head and shook it.

Galen gazed into the sky. "Judging by the wind, it will be almost two ninedays until we reach the Citadel. We must be as ready as we can be. Rather, you must be."

Frowning, I said, "Ready for what?"

Galen scoffed. "You cannot know the peril into which you go. Training at the Citadel is dangerous for an elf. Deaths during the process are rare but not unheard of. You are not an elf, as you know. I may have the Emperor's permission to make a human Bladeguard, but I do not have the support of others in his council, nor others at the Citadel. There are greater tests that await you, if you can survive them."

"If it's dangerous, then why not train me in the sword? That's why you're called a Bladeguard, right?"

"We are trained experts in the sword, correct. But that is not why the Emperor gave us the name. We are his blades, his weapons against his enemies. As you will be, if you are chosen."

I sighed. My heart sank. What would I have to do to be chosen?

"Every Bladeguard was trained to be the weapon," Galen said, "before we were given a sword. I am training you the same, Caleb. You will be the weapon I forge. The sword will only be an extension of your heart, if you believe you have one. Do you understand?"

I raised my eyes and met his stare. "Yes."

"Good. Now continue. Push-ups. How many yesterday?"

My arms were already made of rubber. But they had been the day before, too. "A hundred and fifty."

Galen grinned. "Yes. Two hundred today. Begin."

Lyne brought me dinner as I lay in the bunk in my cabin. Flatbread, bosaur jerky, and an apple. The room was dark but for a small candle.

I groaned when I sat up. "Thank you."

Setting the iron plate on the bed before me, she gave a curt nod and produced a salve from the folds of her brown dress.

My eyes bulged. I took it from her. "You're a lifesaver."

Lyne's grin didn't break the continual look of sadness about her. She began to leave the room.

"Have you been to the Citadel?" I asked.

She paused at the door and didn't look back when she spoke. "Yes."

"Is it as he says?" I took a strip of jerky. "Dangerous? Deadly?"

The wood of the ship croaked, and waves whispered from above. She sniffed. "The Bladeguard train to be the greatest warriors in the world. That is dangerous. Violent."

I took a bite of the jerky. "You know, I lived on a farm, long ago, with my Da and Ma."

Lyne turned her body and regarded me.

"We mostly grew crops," I said, "but we also had some animals for meat. Chickens. Pigs. We had this one pig, and I remember that Da would feed the pig and check on it every day, for months. Da fed it our trash, leftovers, nasty stuff. The pig grew bigger and bigger until the time came." I snorted. "He walked right up to the pig one day. The pig looked up at him. Da met the animal's stare and then bashed its head in with a wooden staff.

"We cleaned and ate that pig for weeks."

Lyne's brow creased.

"I got that feeling today." I chewed and swallowed down the bite of salty jerky. "Like I was the pig, being fed, given salves to heal, just to start again the next day. Is that true, you think? Am I right? Am I the pig to Galen?"

Lyne averted her eyes and took a deep breath. "Nothing for it now. Get some rest. You will need it."

CHAPTER 11

BLADES FOR WINGS

The morning began with a mist, making it difficult to see far from the ship. Once the sun rose higher in the sky, the fog dissipated, and off in the distance, a series of towers reached for the clouds. The towers were smooth, white stone, as if made by the gods. When we grew near, I made out five towers, each coming to a point, the one closest to the ocean the thickest and highest, windows designating different levels.

At the root of the towers was a series of buildings, domes with arches and covered walkways between. The complex was like a small city and surrounded by a high wall. The structures and walls were made of the same white stone.

The Citadel.

The mist burned away while the clean, white towers grew closer, making the Citadel appear like a paradise in the clouds, a majestic home of supernatural beings, immortal and incorruptible.

But I knew what lived there. Death. They trained elves in the various ways of assassination and strategy, manipulation and power over others. Those elves were the ultimate weapon of the Emperor, and humanity his primary target.

The wind whipped my hair, and I turned my face into it, my eyes never leaving the Citadel.

Lyne leaned against the railing next to me. "What do you think?"

I narrowed my eyes. "It's beautiful."

"Yes."

"Am I allowed to say it scares the crit out of me?"

Lyne chuckled. "The Citadel has been my home for many years. It is not a place that welcomes our kind."

"Humans."

She nodded. "Those halls and towers are designed to cause fear, in their own way, however beautiful. I'm sure they want us afraid, so you are allowed."

Still holding onto the railing of the ship, I stood to my full height, resolving to not feel that fear, to not surrender to that hand of Tablets. With the Citadel growing larger in my vision, it didn't really work.

Galen joined us on the deck, his white hair tied behind him and flapping in the breeze. "Grab your things. It is time."

The Last Sentinel drew near the long pier extending from the Citadel, and other ships were moored there, both larger and smaller. Our boat docked easily, the crew working with expert precision.

I had grabbed my bag – only a few changes of clothes – and stood on the deck when the ramp was lowered down to the dock. Galen descended the ramp first, then I followed, Lyne after me. She carried far more than I did, so I grabbed a couple of her packs, too, once we stood on the pier. Galen carried nothing except a sword at his belt.

Two humans hustled past us back up the ramp. They both bore the eagle tattoo on their wrist, a sign of slavery in the Kryan Empire. While they averted their eyes with Galen, one of them flashed a glance at me, a strange mixture of fear and curiosity in his eye.

I stumbled at the look and skipped to catch up with Galen.

Galen led us toward the shore and a path through high stone and rock before we entered the complex through a high arch in the wall, thick golden doors open wide. We continued along the path, white cobblestone under our feet, until we came to a massive, domed building, what appeared to be the center of the complex.

"I need to take those packs back now," Lyne said. "Thank you."

"Sure." I shifted the ones I took from her off my shoulder and gave them to her as gently as I could. "Will I see you again?"

Lyne grinned. "I'm sure. Good luck to you, Caleb."

I returned a smile. "Thanks."

"Come," Galen said with a sharp tone, and I rushed to catch up with him.

A huge eagle made of gold decorated the doors of the central building, and when I grew closer, the wings of the eagle were not made of feathers but golden, curved blades.

Four slaves opened those doors, and we made our way into an expansive front hall. Tapestries covered the interior walls interspersed with oil lamps. Our steps made whispering echoes.

An elf stood in the midst of the hall. Slightly shorter than Galen, he had long, straight auburn hair. His robe was simple blue and embroidered at the hem with gold. He bowed to Galen and placed a hand on the hilt of the fine, curved sword at his hip.

"Master Galen," the elf said. "The Citadel welcomes you."

Galen gave a slight nod. "Iletus. It is good to be back."

Iletus inclined his head toward me. "I see you found another for your experiment."

My brow creased. "Another?"

Galen stood still a moment while Iletus raised a brow at me, like I wasn't allowed to speak.

"He was quite the discovery." Galen addressed the elf, ignoring my question. "I will relay the story to you later. Are the others at breakfast?"

"If not, I can have them summoned," Iletus said.

Galen sniffed. "It has been a long journey, and I believe this boy is hungry. Let us see if the others are there. After breakfast, we must show him to his room."

"Of course." Iletus spun on a heel and glided toward the far door and a long hallway. Galen and I followed.

I drew close to him. "There are others? Other humans you want to train like me?"

"As I said, this is an opportunity for you." Galen didn't turn, his voice soft but firm. "But it is not a guarantee that we will train you. You must be tested further, and you have competition."

"Competition?" I scoffed. "How many others?"

We walked down the wide hallway, imposing doors spaced out on either side of us.

"There are two other boys."

"And they're already here?"

"Yes."

My chuckle wasn't one of mirth. "That seems unfair. They have an advantage."

"Who told you this was going to be fair?" Galen took a breath. "Whoever is chosen will be thrown into a nest of hungry griders. We must make a wise choice."

I bared my teeth. "So only one of us will be chosen?"

Galen's green eyes turned to me, cold and intense. "Or none."

"And if none of us makes the cut?"

Galen turned forward once more. "Then we shall keep looking. Everything hinges on making the right choice."

I scowled. "And if we aren't the right choice, let me guess, we die?"

Galen nodded. "Very good. You are beginning to understand."

Chapter 12

The Others

Galen and I followed Iletus through a door to the right at the end of the long corridor. Soon we descended a winding staircase that took us into a dark hallway at the bottom.

More human slaves with the eagle tattoo on their wrist bustled about. We passed a laundry room and storage and other areas on our left and right. The hall opened to a spacious room dimly lit with a couple torches in each corner. Tables and chairs were strewn about, a cafeteria of sorts, where the humans took their meager meals.

The slaves eyed me, much like the ones on the dock had, which now made more sense given two other boys had been here for a time before me, the possibility of humans becoming Bladeguard.

It was easy to pick out the other two boys among them. One was Liorian with darker skin. The other had lighter skin like mine, likely from the region of Erelon to the north. Tin plates sat before them, only crumbs remaining. I wasn't surprised when Iletus brought me to their table, and we stopped there, spreading out.

Galen stepped forward and gestured to me. "This is Caleb." He waved to the Liorian. "Mande." Then he pointed at the one with lighter skin. "And Franz."

I took a deep breath. My competition, as it were. I joined Galen and stuck my hand out to Mande. "Well met."

Mande's brow creased, and he grunted, looking away.

Franz rose from his chair and grabbed my hand. He smiled at me. "Caleb. Well met." Franz stood almost a head taller than me and more muscular, his handshake strong. He seemed a year or two older.

I returned the smile, although my jaw tightened.

Franz released my hand.

"Your instructions today are simple," Galen said. "Rest and eat well. Your first test is tomorrow. We leave at the break of day."

Mande narrowed his eyes at Galen.

I glanced from Mande to Galen. "What test?"

"You will have the details tomorrow." Galen nodded to the boy from Erelon. "Caleb, Franz will show you to your room. We will meet here at dawn."

I glanced around the underground room. "How are we supposed to know when the sunrise is?"

Galen raised a brow. "Be here." He turned and left, Iletus in his wake.

Mande watched the two elves leave the cafeteria then bore his gaze into mine. He also appeared a couple years older than me. I met his stare with my own. Mande snorted, stood, and left the cafeteria without a word.

Franz peered after him then shrugged. "Not a happy citizen of the Empire, that one." He faced me. "You hungry?"

"I could eat."

Franz raised a hand and snapped at a younger woman in the corner by an opening to the kitchen beyond. She started and raised her gaze. "Get our friend here a plate," Franz said.

The young woman rushed into the kitchen, to comply, I supposed.

I frowned. "She seems ... frightened of you. All of them do."

"Frightened of *us*," Franz said.

"Why?"

Franz scoffed. "Is it really hard to understand? We're not a secret around here. We don't have the tattoo on our wrist, not expected to act as slaves. We could be trained as Bladeguard, and the slaves here know better than anyone who those elves are, what they are capable of. That scares them."

I nodded. "I guess."

We sat at the table, and the young woman brought me a plate of thick bread, white cheese, and carrots. Franz explained while I ate how he had been taken by Galen in Asya, the largest city in the human lands, and brought to the Citadel a month ago. Mande from Lior had already been at the Bladeguard complex. They had been following a routine of physical exercise set by Iletus.

"Don't mind Mande," Franz said. "He don't talk much to anyone."

I hesitated. "What about ... your family?"

Franz stiffened. "What about them?"

"Did you have to leave them behind?"

"Look, Caleb," Franz said. "Galen gave us the same choice as you. We don't talk about our families since we had to leave them behind. Not to mention we don't want to give anything away and get them on some Bladeguard's list. That goes for all the slaves here in the compound."

I nodded. "Yeah. Okay. What about those Bladeguard? Have you seen many?"

Franz shook his head. "Only Galen and Iletus. And believe me those crit buckets are enough. We stick with the humans down here and have a separate yard for exercise out near the cows and bosaur."

I finished my food in a few more moments, and Franz led me down the next hallway, where Mande went. These were small bedrooms, many with two or more beds within, barely larger than the closet Carys and I had inhabited back in Landen at the shoemaker's. Tattered blankets served as a covering for the entrances. He stopped at one room and gave a mock bow.

"This is your room," Franz said. "Mine is across the hall. Mande is next to you here."

I stepped into the tiny room. Only a bed, table, and candle within.

Franz pointed at the bed. "The crit pan is there underneath. For anything more extensive, as far as washing and things, there's a bath down the hall."

"Got it." I threw my bag at the foot of the narrow bed. "So we're just supposed to stay here all day and night? We can't go anywhere?"

Franz lifted and lowered his shoulders. "You can explore a bit if you like, but I wouldn't go far, definitely stay here in the slave quarters."

"What are you going to do?"

"Me?" Franz smiled, but his eyes were cold. "You know what's gonna happen tomorrow, right?"

"A test."

"A test. Right." The smile disappeared. "The test is a competition, the one Mande and I have been waiting for more than a month to do. Since we're humans, it'll likely be a test that can kill us. What am I gonna do? I'm gonna wait and rest, like Galen said."

I glanced up and down the hallway. "All day?"

"You'll see us at lunch and dinner," Franz said. "Otherwise, you know where I'll be."

Franz took a few steps over to the door to his room, swept the blanket aside with one arm, and he paused there.

"Remember," he said to me. "Tomorrow? We ain't friends. We ain't gonna be helping each other. You seem like a great kid, but it's about survival. Nothing personal."

Franz ducked into his room.

I blew a deep breath out of my lungs.

After sitting in that dark, stifling room, I did go out and explore the basement area where the human slaves lived. I didn't see any children, and the slaves bustled around at various tasks. Other hallways branched off the main, and the warren-like nature of the connections was confusing at first. An hour later, I had the basic idea of the layout and marking points designated.

Headed back to my room, I passed Lyne.

She paused, and her face brightened. She was the only slave that didn't either look away or cower when I passed.

"Are you well?" she asked me.

"Yeah, fine," I said. "Just bored."

Lyne chuckled. "Can I get you anything?"

I paused. "Maybe something to read? Not sure if that's allowed."

"I'll bring you what I can. Will you be in your room?"

I nodded. "You know where it is?"

"I do." She smiled before walking away.

Another hour later, she arrived at my room, pulling back the curtain and handing me a book. "Galen chose this for you."

I took the heavy tome from her. "Contigus."

"Yes. I must go." Lyne left the room.

More essays from this philosopher and historian. I moved closer to the candle next to the bed and began to read.

Chapter 13

The Living Mountain

The three of us stood high on a ledge on the mountain behind the Citadel. Franz, Mande, and I were spaced evenly a few mitres from a wall of rock. Galen and Iletus stood behind us.

"This is Mount Vivamo," Galen said. "She is the legend of the living mountain. The elder elves believed she gave birth to one of the gods and became the foundation of the Kryan Kingdom, what is now our great empire."

I hadn't slept well, even though I read until the candle burned out, and I lay in the dark for most of the night. When I began to hear more movement out in the passageways, I roused, taking that to mean morning was upon us.

Mande and Franz already sat at a table in the cafeteria when I arrived, Galen and Iletus a few minutes later. I hadn't missed the dawn. With few words, the five of us made the trek out a back entrance of the building, through the complex, and started the steep climb to the mountain.

Now here we were on a flat shelf of stone staring up at the massive peak. We each wore only thin breeches that extended down past our knees. Barefoot and bare-chested, I shivered.

"Your first obstacle is to climb to the next ledge above," Galen continued. "There you will find the mouth of a cave. You will enter the cave and find your way to the other side of the mountain. The first two of you to make it will continue with the next test. One way or another only two of you will survive."

Galen paused, and I fought the urge to glance back at the elf or the other boys.

"If only one survives?" Franz asked.

"This is the first of two tests," Galen said. "Even if only one survives, then he must still face the second quest."

My jaw tightened. "If none of us survive?"

"Then we keep searching," Galen said. "This first test is the same for all those who train to be Bladeguard."

Franz caught my eye before he peered over his shoulder. "And the second?"

"Worry about this test," Galen said. "For today, nothing else exists."

Franz scowled and faced forward once more.

"When I say the word, you will start." Galen hesitated, and I took a deep breath, my gaze searching for my initial hand and footholds. "Begin."

All three of us leapt forward to separate parts of the wall. I needed to jump to find purchase with my right hand, straining to lift a bit for my foot to find a good spot.

Long ago, as a child with my father, we lived near the base of the mountains. Da had taught me to climb a bit over rocks and ledges when the time allowed. But that had been years ago.

As physical or athletic as I thought I was, climbing up a wall of stone exhausted me within moments. One hand and foot at a time, straining to lift and make it the next mitre, sweat covered my body, and there among the whipping wind, my almost continual shivering didn't help.

With a glance, Franz was ahead of me and Mande behind. Our grunts echoed off the mountain, sounding distant, however close we were.

My toes were wedged in a crack, then slipped, and due to the sudden extra weight on my left hand, I lost that hold. I reached and snagged a horn of rock above my head with my right hand, and I dangled there for a split second, my feet scrambling for purchase. My left foot found one, and I had to stretch out with my left hand to grab the original hold.

Freezing in the cold and open air, I paused with heaving breaths, my heartbeat pounding, my eyes closed.

Once I opened my eyes, my slip had cost me. Both boys were ahead of me now, and gritting my teeth to keep them from chattering in the chill, I hauled myself up and onward.

Franz reached the edge first, swinging his leg up and over while the rest of the body followed. Mande was next, pulling himself with both hands to his waist and scrambling to safety above.

I was only a few seconds behind, and I found a nice hold for my left foot, my toes grasping well, and with my hands on the ledge I tumbled up and onto the flat, rocky area there.

Franz and Mande already approached the mouth of a cave ten mitres away. I paused on my hands and knees for a moment, trying to catch my breath, then jumped to my feet and followed. While I moved, my legs and arms felt weak and fluid.

Great, I thought. *I'm only at the beginning, behind, and it hurts to move.*

Once in the cave, the sun provided some light, but that quickly diminished. As my eyesight adjusted, Franz held a burning torch up ahead, Mande grabbing one, too. I rushed forward to latch onto the third one, but Mande grabbed it with his other hand and tossed it off to his left, into the shadows and away from me.

"What the shog're you doing?" I screeched.

Mande gave me a scowl and pushed forward. The light followed them, leaving me in the dim back part of the cave. My growl echoed off the rock around me, and I hustled over toward my fading torchlight. Grabbing the torch, the flame had died down but not extinguished.

I cursed and raced into the narrow passageway where Franz and Mande went. Once within, their torches bounced ahead through the tunnel winding to the right and down.

The air was suddenly warmer while we descended deeper into the mountain, the scent of something familiar. A red-orange glow began to wait for us at the other end of the tunnel, faint at first but then stronger.

The tunnel dumped us out onto another flat rocky area that ended in a pit. The red-orange glow came from the bottom of the pit, and another ledge waited for us on the other side. I recognized the familiar scent now, fire and sulfur.

Franz arrived at our edge first. Attached to stalagmites were three ropes hung from up above in the dark. The only way over.

With barely a hesitation, Franz shifted his torch to his left hand and swept one of the ropes into his right. He was bigger, taller, but that didn't seem to affect his speed or agility. Franz leapt from the edge, and he hung onto the rope and swung over the pit.

Drawing closer, the pit was filled with lava.

Not a mountain, after all. A volcano. Living. The sounds of molten rock churned below us.

Mande was next, a few mitres ahead of me, and he did pause for a moment to take a rope and throw it over the pit without him.

My jaw dropped. "What the break …?" I sprinted forward.

Then Mande took the other rope in his hand, pushed back on a stalagmite with both feet, arcing back and then hefting his feet back and forward to give him momentum while he swung over the pit, his own torch still in his hands as he swung.

I lunged with my arms to grab his waist, my only hope for getting across, but my fingers slipped off his sweat-covered skin. I almost fell headfirst into the pit, flailing and grabbing one of the stalagmites, and my right foot hung over the massive lava hole for a split second.

Mande sailed over the pit.

Franz had already landed on the other side, torch still in his hand, wrapping his rope around a stone. He didn't even look back while he continued into another cavern.

Mande landed three ticks of time later.

I yelled in frustration, and my whole body went rigid in anger. No time to rail and rant now. Had to get across. I took a breath and looked up. The first rope that Mande had loosed swirled directly over the pit. However, Mande hadn't tied his rope to a stone or stalagmite on the other side.

That rope started to swing back toward me.

Had he been so concerned with Franz that he messed up? Did it matter?

I hurried a retreat, keeping focused on the rope. I would have to time this perfectly. My bare feet shuffled on the stone. The rope passed the center of the pit and wiggled toward me.

Running with all my speed, the faint torch in my hand waved with my arm, and at the very end of the ledge, I vaulted myself with all my might across and over the lava pit, reaching out with my right hand. The rope slowed and hung there at my palm. My fingers closed over it, my eyes bulging, and I gripped it.

The rope started to slip out of my sweaty hand.

I cried out and had to drop the torch so I could grab the rope with my left hand to stop my descent. Now the rope was in both hands, and I kicked my legs out forward with all my might and swung toward the other side.

The hot air blew past my bare chest and face while the far edge rushed at me. Because I had slipped down the rope, I would arrive low ... if I would get there at all since I didn't have a full swing. I judged the apex of my swaying motion, and using as much momentum as I could, I released the rope and twisted in the air, my arms and legs thrashing about. My body went almost horizontal, and my hands caught on the lip of the ledge, which meant the rest of me slammed into the jagged stone, like a dozen rock punches at once.

I barely held on, but I did. The collision had knocked the breath out of me, and I had to wait until I could suck air into my lungs again, coughing and spitting.

I was too far behind. I had to move.

Despite the better footing due to the jagged stone, I was slow getting over the lip and onto the ledge.

My jaw tightened and my eyes narrowed. Fists hung at my side. I was bleeding in several places – my cheek and chest – but I didn't care.

I blew out air through my teeth and sprinted into the pitch-black cavern ahead without a torch.

CHAPTER 14

IT'S NOT PERSONAL

The dark. The heat. The pain. I tried to make friends with it all, accepting the agony and anger as fuel.

I moved as fast as I could with my hands out in front of me at an angle, feeling my way forward. My shoulder hit the side of the tunnel when it made a sharp turn. I appreciated being only in my breeches, soaked in sweat from the stifling heat.

A few more mitres ahead, I could make out another red-orange glow. I quickened my pace since the dim light penetrated the darkness, and soon I emerged into another large open area with thick columns of rock, natural and irregular shapes. While the light was low, I could make out the barriers and did my best to continue onward.

I was far behind the other two, but I had to push that concern out of my mind. The random shapes and placement of rock columns confused me, and soon I lost my direction like a child in an unknown forest.

My father had taught me how to move when lost in a forest, but the success of that depended upon sunlight or stars or moon, a fixed point in the sky I could use to navigate or use as an origin of some kind.

First, my father had instructed me to make sure I was calm, refusing to make any decisions out of desperation or panic. Fear corrupted any choice, and so I closed my eyes for a moment and took a deep breath.

Then a fist struck me in the side of the head.

I reeled, and the world spun around me. Disoriented, I stumbled and covered by head with my arms. Another punch landed on my ribs and midsection. My shoulder struck stone, a column, and I slid down and rolled aside.

There was a sound of flesh hitting rock, and a voice cried out. My vision cleared, and when I stepped back, there was the boy, holding his hand and squinting in pain.

"Mande!" I said. "Why?"

That was a dumb question. So dumb Mande didn't answer, not that I ever heard him say a word.

This wasn't a game or a competition of skill. Someone was going to die, and Mande had decided I would be the one that didn't survive.

Mande bared his teeth and came at me again.

I sidestepped his attack, my feet sliding over while I leaned away from his punch. I lifted my right foot and sent it into his crotch. Hard.

Not very nice, I know. But I didn't want to waste any more time. I had to try and catch Franz.

My heel had driven into his groin, a precise Sand-bol type kick.

Mande's frown shifted into a grimace, his open mouth soundless but it looked like a scream. He fell to the rock floor in a ball.

I peered upwards and found a fixed point – a stalactite situated back toward the tunnel I just exited – and I now moved away from that point in a general direction around and past columns of rocks until sounds reached my ears, swelling noises that rumbled and roared.

Circling the final column of stone, there was a flat area and another gaping pit. However, this time a narrow stone bridge stretched before me across the chasm. The walkway appeared at least 75 mitres from this side of the pit to the other.

The ground shook beneath me, and my brow furrowed. I stepped a few paces closer to the edge of the chasm and paused in horror while the lava erupted from beneath, surging upward to the top of the pit.

The horror wasn't for the lava alone, though. There were shapes within the lava, squirming things. I squinted. The shapes were like snakes but thicker, each of them a sickly yellow with a gaping maw at one end and rows of teeth. They were worms. In the lava.

The lava worms were each as long as the span of my arm, and they bounded up out of the lava like they had been swimming and landed on the stone bridge, hundreds of them at a time, covering it, their mouths snapping and chewing at air.

After a few moments, the churning lava receded. A good portion of the lava worms remained and wiggled about, but after another set of seconds they launched themselves off the walkway and back into the lava below.

That was the way forward.

I found no sign of Franz. The other side of the walkway was filled with shadow. If he was there, he was beyond my sight. Perhaps he fell down into the pit.

I swallowed hard. Then I cursed myself.

I should have been counting ... something. Heartbeats, seconds, using a measure to determine how much time I would have to get across.

The ground rumbled. The lava erupted. Once the liquid fire reached the top of the pit, I began counting, and eight heartbeats later, the lava abated. I counted the next set. Another eight heartbeats until the ground rumbled and the lava rose.

Could I make it over 75 mitres in that amount of time? I would have to.

I was on heartbeat four and watching the segmented lava worms rolling over the stone bridge when a scuffling sound came from behind me, barely audible amidst the grumbling lava and squeaks from the worms.

Casting a glance over my shoulder, Mande rested a second on the rock pillar nearest me, his face a snarl. He still held his crotch, but he gathered his strength to rush me.

I still counted in my head, and on eight, I faced back to the walkway and took off.

Mande ran after me.

The walkway burned the bottom of my feet, but that only increased my motivation to push myself at top speed while I counted, the sound of pounding steps behind.

I was at the count of five and only halfway across the walkway. Perhaps in the dark I had misjudged the distance at 75 mitres; either that or between the climb, heat, near death across the first pit, and Mande's attack, my body wasn't as fast as usual.

Whatever the case, the bridge began to shake, the odd sound of lava bubbling and squeaking from the terrible lava bugs wafted with the increased heat. I shortened and quickened my steps, but I didn't seem to go any faster.

I wasn't going to make it.

On count seven, I was still a good ten mitres from the far edge, and the lava with seething worms swirled just beneath me. I hit count eight and leapt forward with all the strength I had left, sailing across the last couple mitres.

I landed on my face and chest where the walkway met the other side of the chasm, and in my fear and desperation, my feet, knees, and hands tore at the stone beneath me until I was another few paces beyond the walkway, far enough that I thought I was safe.

Mande had been right behind me.

Looking back with wide eyes to the walkway, I sat up on my haunches, my hands on my knees, my breath heaving.

Mande had almost made it. Somehow the boy had closed the distance between us and had only been a few paces behind when the lava worms crested the walkway. This time, his scream wasn't silent while the large worms with thick, segmented bodies bit into his legs. He kicked and struggled, and a few of them fell away … but not all. Mande crawled forward, straining on his hands and elbows, his hands clawing for purchase while the burning worms attacked him.

This was the boy who tried to take advantage and leave me behind, even attacked me only moments before. I should have enjoyed watching him suffer – didn't he deserve it? – but his face that once only scowled with anger was now a mask of terror and pain, his screams begging me for help.

With a deep growl, I scrambled forward and reached out. He grabbed my hand. I hadn't been counting, forgotten as I reached the relative safety. I took his one hand in both of mine and pulled with all my might. He landed beside me, a distance away from the stone bridge, and he turned over on his back, sobbing.

I also lay on my back, gulping sulfuric air and coughing.

Sitting up with one last hack from my lungs, I looked over at Mande.

Most of his breeches had been singed away, and small chunks of his burned legs were missing, bitten away by those worms.

"Can you walk?" I said.

Mande slowly sat up and looked at his burnt and injured legs. "I don't know."

I made it to my feet. "Come on. I can try and help you to the next tunnel at least."

A voice sounded from the darkness. "Leave him."

Mande and I both turned our heads to see Franz emerge from the shadows.

"What?" I scoffed. "We can't leave him here."

Franz gestured toward the tunnel. "This was the last part. The test is over. There's daylight on the other side of that tunnel. He lost."

I sighed. "Fine, but that doesn't mean we have to leave him here."

The ground began to rumble, the lava making its way back to the top.

Mande turned over on his side and pushed to his knees. "No. I can make it."

Franz stepped closer while Mande struggled to his feet. Mande hissed and grunted in pain, but he did stand. Barely.

Franz shook his head. "You know what this means."

Mande lowered his head.

"Hey, wait," I said. "We know what it means to those elves out there. It doesn't have to control what we do in here."

Mande lifted his gaze to mine, a curious look.

The lava raised to the top, the lava bugs squirming within.

Franz stood next to me now and narrowed his eyes at me. Then with a move fast and strong, he shoved Mande back to the walkway that was again covered in those lava bugs.

Mande's injured legs betrayed him while his body flew backward, his hands and arms extending for assistance that never came. The boy landed among the worms, and they covered his chest and legs. They feasted.

My hand reached out, and I froze there a few seconds with my mouth hanging open. I recovered, blew a breath, and turned to Franz, my hands now in fists at my side, waiting for him to do the same to me.

Franz frowned. "Like I said, it's not personal."

He pivoted on a heel and walked away and toward the tunnel beyond.

Chapter 15

Reasons to Win

Franz hadn't lied. Daylight awaited us at the other end of that tunnel.

He killed Mande. Another boy. Another human.

Elves killed humans. We weren't supposed to kill each other.

But wasn't that the purpose of this experiment, as Galen called it? They would take a human and train him to think and fight like an elf, to infiltrate human society, find the pockets of rebellion and root out those the elves deemed traitors to their perfect empire. That Bladeguard would be human on the outside but an elf within.

The fact had existed in my brain before that day, but after seeing Franz push Mande back onto the walkway to be killed by those disgusting lava bugs, the reality of it settled on my heart, my soul.

I had been abducted, given little choice but to participate, and I had justified my decision by committing to use this training to learn my enemy and destroy the Empire from within. I even had an idea of a pithy prophecy to help me with that.

But now it had changed. I could see the danger in what Galen attempted. With Franz, the elves could accomplish the goal, to have a human who thought and killed as an elf. What would happen when a human Bladeguard like that was unleashed upon humanity?

A Bladeguard like Franz could find his way into any city and begin talking about his faith in El, a little at first, just hints, and it might take a few months, but eventually he'd get invited to a meeting. He'd pretend to be interested in the message, in the words, and if he was patient enough, a crazy old man would come to town and the whispers would begin of the legend, the Prophet.

Trained by the deadliest warriors in the world, he would now be able to kill the Prophet. And his wife Kendra. And his son Earon.

And a little girl named Carys.

Even if both Franz and I died here, Galen would find someone to do his bidding, the command of the Empire. With what I had just seen with Franz and Mande, it was clear.

I no longer had to win to survive, or to kill elves, at least not those reasons alone. Now I needed to win and become the Bladeguard so the Empire wouldn't have a weapon like Franz at their disposal.

The air cleared with less sulfur, and it cooled while the white light of day began to give a hint ahead. We emerged from the tunnel, Franz first. I followed, squinting and shading my eyes against the sun.

Galen and Iletus stood there, their hair and robes waving in the wind. Neither reacted when we stopped and faced them.

Galen measured us with his stare and addressed Franz. "Mande?"

"He didn't make it." Franz said.

Galen nodded. "Very well."

Without a care that a boy had just died, the elves turned and walked down the mountain path. Franz started after them. I took one last look back at the tunnel into the mountain, and then I walked the path with weakened limbs, burning and painful feet, and a weighted heart.

I bathed down the hall in the slaves' quarters, the water turning tepid, but I soaked there anyway for a good amount of time. Moving to my room, oils and salves waited for me, reminding me of Landen and how I left my family.

After dressing in a tunic and clean pants, I lay on my bed in the dark. I had just begun to drift off to sleep when there was movement at the blanket across my door.

"The master has asked for you," the voice said. Lyne.

"Tell the master I'm asleep," I mumbled with my eyes still closed.

She hesitated. "I would advise against that."

"Whatever." I sat up, muscles and the bottom of my feet still sore. I had to give the elves credit, those oils and salves lessened pain and sped the healing process, preparing me like the pig.

Lyne led me through the slave quarters and then up the stairs to the main building where we wove up other stairs to a higher floor. Lyne asked after my injuries, and I gave her curt answers. It wasn't her fault, though. I wasn't in the mood.

Soon we ascended a winding staircase in one of the towers, up to the top. She smiled and left me at a simple but tall door. I forced a grin back at her.

The door had the Citadel emblem upon it, the golden eagle with blades for wings.

With a breath, I collected myself and entered the door.

The expansive room had a high roof but was sparsely decorated. Galen sat in a comfortable chair at a desk. He didn't look up when he spoke. "Caleb. Sit."

Three other chairs faced him on the other side of the desk, also padded. I chose the one furthest away from him and sat.

The elf put down his pen and raised his gaze. "I trust you are recovering well?"

"I'll live."

"Yes, well, that remains to be seen, doesn't it?"

I frowned.

"Mande," Galen said. "Did you kill him?"

My face went blank. "No."

"Did he die from one of the obstacles?"

With a furrowed brow, I remained silent. Why was he asking me? If he spoke with Franz first, he surely knew already.

I sniffed. "What does it matter?"

"I must have data as we continue this experiment, information regarding not only your physical prowess but your choices, your personality, your intelligence, and more."

"So this is part of the test?"

Galen cocked his head. "Everything you do is part of the test, of course. For us to put trust in a human, that will require a great amount of patience, for both of us. Now answer the question."

My jaw tightened. "He died being eaten by those lava worms, but that's not what killed him."

"Ah. So not you but Franz?"

I nodded. "He killed him."

"If you become a Bladeguard, you will kill many people along the way."

"But this wasn't an enemy. I thought they were friends."

Galen raised a brow. "Why would you think that?"

"They spent time here, together, before I arrived."

The elf's mouth became a line. "I see. I hope that now you've been convinced that assumption was mistaken."

"I guess."

"You need to be sure," Galen said. "To be clear, there are no friends, here. You will find none. No allies. No one on your side among the elves and possibly not the human slaves, either. And when you return to the land of humanity, your job will be to betray many humans you meet. I would not expect to have many friends, if I were you. An elven Bladeguard has few, if any, and a human ...?" He spread his hands at the hopeless nature of the idea.

I took a slow, deep breath. "I think you made yourself clear."

"I am glad," Galen said. "Now, as to the extent of your injuries, nothing appeared broken or too serious. Am I correct?"

I nodded.

"Then you will be ready for the next test tomorrow?" Galen said.

My stare didn't leave his. "I'll be ready."

Galen grinned. "That is excellent. We will see you again before dawn. I believe Lyne will escort you back to your room. I would advise food and as much rest as you can manage."

CHAPTER 16

KATARA ISLE

"That is our destination, the Katara Isle," Galen said, his white hair bound behind him and flapping in the wind while we stood on the deck of *The Last Sentinel.*

The ship lurched up and crashed down after a massive wave. I gripped the railing of the ship and bent my knees to withstand the sudden fall and stop. An island had come into view over the past few minutes, and the crew sailed us right toward it.

Franz and I had asked several times over the last couple hours since dawn about the next and final "test." Galen and Iletus had simply led us to the boat. The ship was crewed by the same two elves from before, and we all now gathered on the deck – me, Franz, Iletus, and Galen. Iletus and Galen wore their long robes with belts at their waist and fine swords that hung at their hips. Franz and I were again only in our knee long breeches.

An hour into the journey across the water, we spotted the island, and Galen began speaking, finally giving the details of what we would face.

"That island?" Franz said.

Galen nodded. "It is also called the island of the Cursed One."

"Great," I mumbled.

"It is a smaller island and once belonged to a great and wealthy wizard," Galen said.

I raised a brow and stood straight. Magic?

Galen turned his face into the wind. "As you know, magic is easily corrupted. But thousands of years ago, the elves celebrated those that had the power of the gods. From the records, great beings of majesty and evil also roamed this world. It was different time."

"Dragons?" I gazed over at the island, high mountains at its center. It seemed to grow as we sailed west. The scriptures of El spoke of dragons ...

Galen turned to me. "Dragons were among them, along with many creatures we only have hints of now. Much has been lost from that time, and even all the elves of that age have passed into memory. The elven wizards were great heroes at first, protecting the common people, elves, dwarves, and humans, from those threats. Over time, however, those elven magicians became twisted in their mind. Those who were the most powerful were called Worldbreakers. It is dangerous when people with great power are also insane."

I swallowed hard and gripped the railing tight.

"A few centuries ago, the human, elven, and dwarven kingdoms made it illegal to practice magic." Galen turned back to the west. "It has been many years since any of those with the ability have developed it, but every now and then we must hunt down an elf who attempts to learn."

Only elves had the ability to do magic, to manipulate the forces of the world with their mind. No other race had the power.

"As I said," Galen continued, "Katara Isle was home to one of the great wizards, back when they were considered heroes. He was also one of the first to begin perverting and pushing his abilities too far. His name was Jeromus.

"Jeromus thought he had figured out how to be immortal, to be invincible and live forever. Jeromus combined elements that should never be interacted with, and he drew too much power within himself. The resulting event was a type of explosion that killed everyone on the island and poisoned the very soil, stone, and water there."

"The Cursed," I said.

"Yes." Galen sighed. "Nothing can ever grow on the island, and the castle and luxurious, prosperous complex is now a ruinous shell. Jeromus got his wish, however, he did become immortal."

Franz glanced from me then back at Galen. "The explosion didn't kill him?"

"It did not." Galen frowned. "Nothing can kill him. Some of the greatest warriors in the history of Kryus have tried and failed. Many have been to Katara and never returned. While he is technically immortal and invincible, it seems he cannot leave the island. Whatever he conjured to keep him living keeps him bound close to the palace."

I squinted at Galen. "And you're sending us there?"

"Jeromus, also called the Cursed, still roams the island," the master elf said. "He was once incredibly wealthy, and there is great treasure there, objects of gold, silver, and more. He has no use for it, but he protects it just the same."

"You want us to kill an invincible elf?" Franz's eyes bulged. "That's the test?"

I shook my head. "No. He wants us to steal something."

Galen inclined his head. "Very good, Caleb. Yes. Your mission is to go into the ruins of his palace, steal something of value, and return to the ship."

"And deal with an immortal wizard," I said.

"My suggestion would be to avoid that at all costs."

The island came into fuller view, a long pier now visible.

Franz sniffed. "What determines the winner of the test?"

"Simple," Galen said. "Whoever returns to the boat first."

We docked at the long wooden pier within the next half hour, the crew tying us at the furthest point.

Galen extended his hand at the dock. "It is time. Begin."

Chapter 17

Falling Deeper

We ran together down the dock toward the rocky shore. A wide path began at the end of the pier, and that road wound up and through boulders and hills.

Franz was older and taller, and he easily outpaced me. He moved ahead by several paces once we reached the road, which still had wagon wheel tracks, as if it had been frozen in time. The grass on either side of the road was brown and stiff. The wind didn't move it at all.

The more we ran forward, the air became thick and heavy, like a storm threatened to sweep away the whole island at any moment, despite the sunny, clear sky, and there was no breeze.

Franz rounded a hill before me, and when I followed, the ruins met us – a stone archway across the road, and beyond that were tall, large buildings made of stone on either side of the road leading to a massive structure at the top of a hill, the palace Galen had talked about. The buildings and palace were without roofs and half of the walls were gone, whether by the explosion Galen spoke about or time or both, I didn't know.

Franz stopped at the archway, and I joined him there. He scanned the buildings and areas ahead, looking for the danger we both felt.

I stepped closer to him and whispered through my panting. "Hey. Listen. We need to work together on this."

Franz turned on me with a scowl. "What are you talking about?"

"Look. They want us against each other, divided. That's what they've done to humans for centuries. But we don't have to participate. We can help each other."

He scoffed. "Haven't you been paying attention? We're fighting to survive, here."

"Have *you* been listening?" I raised my brow. "We're going against an immortal wizard. This is so dangerous, Galen and Iletus are waiting back at the boat, ready to leave at any second. If it's about survival, we need to work together."

Franz chuckled and shook his head. "Not a chance. You barely made it out of the last test alive. If Mande hadn't been so stupid to try and kill you himself, he would have beaten you. You might need me, but I don't need you."

"Maybe. But maybe not. We don't know what we're going to face up there."

He shook his head. "Like I said, it's not personal." He took a deep breath and moved forward in a crouch, his head on a swivel.

I growled and leaned against the archway for a few more moments, watching Franz head to the right, using the buildings as cover. With my own deep breath, I went to the ruins at the left, moving from shadow to shadow, keeping my head down and ready for anything.

Every building I moved past, I searched within for a moment for any items of treasure. No way I would be that fortunate, but I had to try. They were empty shells.

Franz made his way toward the palace, which seemed the likeliest place for any silver or gold, and the best place to find a crazy, powerful wizard.

Closer to the palace, other objects dotted the ground, like deteriorated wooden buckets and rusted iron tools strewn about. A part of me thought of grabbing one of the common hammers and running back to the boat, but no way Galen would count those as treasure.

Tightening my jaw, I crept toward the front door of the palace, which had once been a cast iron gate but was now twisted and torn by some fierce force, a power I didn't want to encounter.

Franz had already gone before me. I could see his bare footsteps in the dust and ash on the cracked marble floor in the spacious entryway. I went to the right into what seemed a ballroom. Patterns in the floor peeked through the dirt and grime, and broken colored glass covered the ground in front of the high, empty windows along the northern side of the building.

Barefoot, I did my best to pick my way through the ballroom and found my way into a hallway down the center of the palace. Again, hints of common objects littered the hallway and rooms, but nothing of treasure. I approached a thick, wooden door half opened, a bright area beyond it.

I made no sound, sneaking up to the door. I gave the door a gentle push with my fingertips. I caught a glimpse at the vast room within, domed with big, irregular holes in the roof, the sun beaming through.

The ancient hinges squeaked like wounded mice while the door opened. The area past the door seemed empty, as well, so I forced it open another few centimitres.

And a series of detritus cascaded down all around me. I cried out and covered my head with my arms while pieces of wood and iron crashed upon me and the hard floor beneath, stirring up dust and ash. Coughing, I ducked and rolled into the room.

Within a few seconds, I had made a great deal of noise, and the clamor echoed through that room, the hallway behind me, and the whole palace.

Once the garbage stopped falling, I looked up and swore. Someone had wedged those items above the door, a type of trap.

Franz.

All that noise would have woken the dead. Or an immortal wizard.

I stood and wiped the ash from my face. "Not personal, huh?" I muttered and cleared my throat. "Feels pretty breakin' personal."

Lightning flashed above the dome, sparking across the cloudless, blue sky.

Slowly, I looked up. My shoulders slumped.

The wind picked up through the holes in the wall and the roof.

"Well, break me," I whispered.

A whistling, whooshing sound came first, then a figure came crashing through the roof, wood splintering and shattering in all directions. I crossed my arms once more over my eyes, and shards of wood and stone peppered me like small arrows.

The figure landed in the middle of the room with a deafening boom, and the ground shook. The whole palace shook.

I looked up. I took a step back.

The being before me wasn't completely elven.

Parts of him were. The right side of his face, chest, and arm were white flesh and recognizable as an elf. The left side of his face was more like a lizard with red and green scales, white pus oozing from between the loose scales. The left half of his mouth was larger than the rest, and the teeth there black and protruded like fangs. His right arm was larger than the other, muscular and also covered in scales, the end a claw with talons.

Both eyes were solid black. Lifeless.

The bottom part of him was opposite – the left leg was more like elven flesh, however thin and emaciated. The right limb shorter but thicker and covered with scales and ending in a larger version of the claw.

One black horn extended from the lizard part of his head, curved and pointed. On the other part of his skull, above his eye, fragments of his brain were exposed through openings in his skull, and those sections of pink matter throbbed like a heartbeat, glistening with something wet.

He wore nothing, the complete abomination visible.

The Cursed.

I froze for a split moment, taking in the horror before me, the fear binding my every muscle with tension and weakness at the same time.

Then the Cursed being took a slurping breath, and he exhaled with a gurgling noise. His black eyes lifted from the ground until they met my own. His jaw dropped like a hungry, menacing snake, the bottom moving impossibly low, revealing a forked tongue. He sucked in the next rippling breath ... and roared.

The sound was like an earthquake met thunder and the screech of an owl all at once.

The Cursed lifted from his foot and claw and hovered there, his hand and talons extending out next to him, balls of fire circling the end of those limbs. He flew at me.

I could move, then.

I spun on my heel and raced back into the hallway where I came from, forcing my breath to catch and get some air while my arms and legs pumped with all my might, my eyes wide.

The door behind me exploded in flame, and the Cursed followed, the roar and screech more like a pulse, rising and falling in volume. I fought the urge to fall on the ground and become a ball like a baby, as well as the desire to look back and see how far behind the creature was. If the sound the Cursed made was any indication, he came faster than I could run.

The wall next to me erupted from some magic ball of fire. I made a squeaking noise, stumbling and somehow staying on my feet. I started shifting back and forth, side to side, making myself more difficult to hit, although that slowed me down.

Still, I was an easy target and needed to get out of the hallway, but if I ducked into a room on either side, would I only be trapped there?

Another ball of fire hit the wall on the other side of the hallway, flames burning my shoulder. The Cursed wasn't a very good shot, but he was coming up fast and would soon be able to reach out and grab me with that claw.

Up ahead, an entrance without a door gave me hope, sunlight beaming through, which hinted at an open window. Open to what, I didn't know, but anything would be better than being caught by that terror.

I faked right, like a Sand-bol move, and then darted left into the room, changing direction on bare feet sliding a bit on the grime on the floor. Once in the room, it was empty with broken tables and one miraculously intact chair.

The window was, in fact, devoid of glass and began about waist high.

I hurtled an old broken table, and when I landed, I reached down and grabbed the back of that chair. At the moment I reached the window, I spun and hurled the chair behind me toward the door.

The Cursed appeared in the doorway and was met with the chair in the face, silencing the screeching roar for a second.

My momentum took me out of the window either way, and I helped it along by jumping off both feet backward through the window.

I twisted mid-air while I fell, curious to see what I had leapt into. A crumbling wooden trap door awaited me a few mitres down, a storage area or garbage chute. I turned at the last moment to hit the wood with my shoulder, crashing through.

The wood slowed my fall a little, but I kept dropping through some type of hole, my stomach nauseous and tight at the weightless feeling. I noted the beam across the narrow pit and tried to adjust my body to miss it with my body. The beam scraped along my upper left chest, and I was able to hook my arm around it, to stop the fall into pitch black.

My arm wasn't strong enough. I slipped from the beam and spilled once more into the darkness and shadow.

In a different story, I would have landed in water or on something soft. You know me well enough to know that's now how my stories go.

I hit something hard, dirt and stone, and lay there motionless, looking up at the circle of light above.

Framed within that circle, the Cursed appeared, blocking the light, and a ball of flame came rushing down the hole, directly at me.

CHAPTER 18

TREASURE IN THE DARK

I turned over, rolling on shoulders and legs, pain shooting through my body, but I managed to get out of the way before the flames landed next to me, far enough that I didn't get burned. The flames gave a sudden burst of light, and the resulting darkness was stark.

Rocks and soil followed the flames, and I scurried out of the way.

I collapsed in agony. It hurt to move, to breathe, and I gave up for a few moments, expecting the Cursed to come flying down the hole to finish me off.

He didn't.

Laying there on my back, my arms at my side, my legs straight, I waited in that odd place of injury where I didn't know how bad it was and didn't want to know, so I just refused to move. I could only wait so long, though, and first tried my arms. Not broken. Bruised and battered, my left arm especially, but not broken.

I shifted my legs next. I had hit my knee at some point in the fall, and the kneecap protested. I sat up and got to my feet. My ribs screamed. A couple might be broken, or I aggravated an older injury from Cityguard in Landen or the Living Mountain. The more I moved my body, I made my own diagnosis. I would be sore for a few years, but I could move. It would simply hurt.

The light from the hole had diminished, and when I gazed up, crud and debris had partially blocked it, only a few rays of light peeking through.

Looking down, wooden pieces I had crashed into lay in a pile, and a few of them were on fire, the flames beginning to die out. I chose the longest one with more of a handhold, used dirt to douse half of the board, and lifted it. Now off the ground, the flame caught more air and continued to burn.

A torch.

Glimpsing up, I couldn't go back that way, through the hole, the opening higher than I could think to jump, and rubble barred it.

There were other noises above, a clanging and clattering from within the palace. Sounded like the Cursed found Franz.

I had to find a way out down here. I cast my makeshift torch around to see remnants of crates and barrels, nothing in them now. A storage area of some kind.

I sighed. I had lost direction, tumbling down the hole. I did the one thing I could and randomly started walking.

Forward. As good a direction as any, right?

The burning wood gave minimal light, so I almost hit the side of the underground space before I saw it. Taking cautious steps, I began to explore and soon discovered piles of trash, the remnants of the contents of the room. The garbage proved useful since I found some old cloth that had somehow survived and wrapped the burning end of the wooden plank. The torch now burned brighter.

Muffled sounds of thunder reached me, dirt disturbed and falling while the basement area shuddered, like a battle took place above. Franz and the Cursed?

One end of the basement slanted downward, and I limped into a deeper cavern. The ground leveled, and after a few more steps, another pile appeared in the bubble of torchlight.

My breath caught. I paused and then extended the torch to get a better view.

Plates, candleholders, jewelry, statues, and other items in a stack higher than my head. They were all made of gold and silver, covered in crud, but when I picked up a platter and wiped it with the palm of my hand, the torchlight gleamed off the gold.

The platter seemed too big to carry around if I needed to move fast, so I picked up a silver candleholder and began to peer about for an escape.

Hobbling forward and to the right of the pile of treasure, another item gleamed white ahead. I squinted and approached it. A white pole leaned against an imposing boulder, and when I stood closer, it was a staff made of ivory or bone. I dropped the candleholder and grabbed the staff, light but strong in my hand.

I held the staff, mesmerized by it for a few seconds, but the odd shape of the boulder stirred my curiosity. Bringing the torch near and examining the massive stone, sections were white, like the staff. With the minimal light of the torch, my brain took a minute to comprehend the form.

It was a skull, caked over from a thousand years in the cavern, buried here. I tracked the long snout and even found a tooth half my height.

... great beings of majesty and evil also roamed this world, Galen had said. *Dragons were among them ...*

Dragons. This was the skull of a dragon.

They had passed into legend, and most people dismissed their existence, interpreting their mention in religious texts as symbolic more than reality. But they had been real.

The cavern trembled, dust and sand falling from the ceiling. Being so far underground, the whole island must be quaking with the battle above. It also hinted that Franz still lived.

If the bulk of the treasure was down here with the skull of a dragon, then it would be difficult for Franz to find anything of value. I might have time.

I only had to find a way out. And there had to be one. An old chute to the basement of the palace couldn't be the only way into an area of treasure and a dragon's skull.

I held the white staff in my left hand, using it as a crutch, and the torch in my right, I started to search the rest of the cavern, shuffling around on my stiff leg. Another minute passed, and I rounded the front of the dragon skull to explore the other side.

The oval opening appeared like an illusion at first, like a perfect hand of Tablets dealt to me. Walking closer, however, the mouth of a tunnel became clear. I didn't know the direction or destination, but I entered the shaft.

My legs protested, but I hurried, the torch out in front, the white staff clicking on the rocky floor. The wide and tall tunnel wound to the left and right then curved far to the left and angled down.

Light appeared, a faint glow, and then the end of the shaft came into view. I emerged from the tunnel onto a plateau near the coast, a stone overhang above my head. I scanned the coast, and to my right, the pier extended out into the ocean, *The Last Sentinel* still docked there, the snapping of its white sails echoing in the wind.

I took a deep breath and bent over at my waist, my hands on my knees. Gathering my strength, I pushed forward along the coast over and around rocks, picking my way through.

Arriving at the road, I turned right and walked down the wooden dock toward the ship. Galen and Iletus stood on the deck near the railing and watched me with cold eyes. I walked up the ramp with the staff as a welcome help, and I joined them on the deck.

I looked around the deck and then at the elves. "Franz?"

"You have won the test, Caleb," Galen said.

My shoulders slumped with relief. I nodded and handed the staff over to Galen.

Galen took it, and his brow furrowed. "*This* is what you found?"

I swallowed hard and leaned against the railing. "Yes."

Galen's head whipped over to stare at Iletus, whose own eyes were wide. Iletus turned to me. "Where did you find this?"

"I fell down a hole, and there was this underground cavern. Treasure and stuff there."

"An ... underground cavern?" Iletus' voice was distant.

"I think there was a dragon skull down there, too." I shook my head. "Whatever it was, it was big. That's where this was."

Iletus faced Galen again. "Now it makes more sense," Iletus said.

Galen nodded, looking down at the staff.

A noise came from behind me, and I twisted at my waist.

Franz sprinted down the road toward us, bounding onto the pier. "Wait! I'm here!" Franz lifted a golden bracelet that glinted in the sun.

As much agony as I felt with broken ribs and sprained knee, I winced at Franz. His hair smoked, singed by flames, and red, blistered welts spotted the skin along his chest, arms, and legs.

His eyes met mine, and he slowed, his hands dropping to his side.

Then a sound came from deeper into the island, a blaring thunderous noise, and a wall of air followed, rousing the dust and lifting small stones as the sudden wind rolled toward us. I grasped the railing while the burst of air swept over us, not enough to knock us over but blew our hair back.

Galen crouched to endure it and rose. "We must leave."

Iletus coughed and turned to the crew. "Shove away from the dock! We're leaving!"

Franz looked over his shoulder. I followed his gaze and a figure heaved up above the ruins of the palace at the center of the island. The form was monstrous and cursed, frightening even as small as it appeared to us now, and it roared like a beast, too loud from a creature so far away.

Then the Cursed began to float toward the coast. Right at us.

Franz cried out and began to sprint again.

The crew had already pulled the ropes from the posts at the pier. One of them started adjusting sails while the other produced a long wooden pole and pushing the boat away from the dock. The ramp fell into the water.

"No!" Franz said.

I leaned over the railing, mouth open at his sudden, desperate bout of speed. Franz raced closer to the edge of the pier.

The Last Sentinel drifted further from the dock, first a few paces, now a mitre, then two.

The Cursed glided to the coastline, his twisted face visible.

Franz groaned and pumped his arms with ferocity. He hit the end of the pier on a full run, leaping and flailing like he swam through the air. He reached out, stretching with one hand and caught the ropes at the side of the ship, his body slamming into the wooden side.

The abomination of elf and creature swooped down and forward in a rush, but he halted right at the coastline, above the boulders there, a boundary of some kind. His hands and feet glowed red and yellow. His black eyes watched us, his mouth a snarl.

The Last Sentinel picked up speed and navigated the waves to increase the distance from the long pier, which put us farther and farther out of range of whatever magic the Cursed could throw at us.

Franz's hands reached the deck, climbing over the lip and to safety. He panted, wheezing.

I slid aside while he approached Galen and handed him the bracelet. Franz wouldn't look at me.

"The palace was bare." Franz heaved in breaths. "Nothing anywhere that I could find. I searched every room. That ... thing chased me all over."

Galen raised the bracelet. "Then where did you find this?"

The deck below us shifted up and down while we made our way across the ocean.

"In an old broken dresser in a room on the highest floor. It was in a drawer."

"I am impressed," Galen said. "Not only that you found the bracelet, but that you survived."

Franz cleared his throat. "Thank you."

"However, as you can see, Caleb has won the test. He arrived before you did." Galen gripped the staff.

Franz lowered his eyes.

Galen hesitated, blinked, then said to Franz, "Kneel."

The boy didn't respond at first, then bent down to his knees.

Iletus stepped forward and drew his sword, a curved silver blade.

My fists clenched, and every muscle tensed.

Iletus rotated and extended the blade at me, hilt first.

I glanced from Iletus to Galen.

"Take the sword, Caleb," Galen said.

My mouth went dry, and I licked my lips. "What?"

Galen stared at me, his face blank but hard. "Take it."

I reached out and took the sword. It was lighter than I imagined.

"Now kill him," Galen said.

I scoffed. "Kill Franz?"

"You won the test," Iletus said. "You have survived. He has not."

The hilt settled into my palm, and it felt natural, like I had been born to hold a sword. I had won the test. I would be trained to be a Bladeguard, learn the elven secrets to destroy the Empire one day. Even if I didn't survive for that purpose, I had kept a killer like Franz from the role, someone who had no problem killing humans.

All I had to do was kill him.

I closed my eyes for a moment, and a memory visited me – my father sitting in his chair, reading from the scriptures of El, his hand passing over the prophecy about a man who would leave and return to the land of humanity to lead a revolution.

I only had to run the blade into Franz's body, into his heart. It would be quick. He deserved it.

And I wanted to do it. I wanted to slide the tip of the sword into his flesh, puncture the skin, feel the resistance, and push the steel forward. And become like the evil I desired to fight.

I opened my eyes and narrowed my eyes at Galen. "No."

Galen cocked his head. "You must. That is part of the test."

"Then I fail." I handed the hilt back to Iletus, who stood still.

"The master has given you a command," Iletus said. "You must kill him."

"No, I don't." I lifted the sword and drove the blade into the wooden deck next to Franz, who flinched. "To be honest, he should win. I fell down a hole and happened to find treasure and a way out. There was no skill or cleverness in that. I ran and scurried like a rat. He kept searching an empty house and avoiding an insane wizard until he completed the mission. That's pretty amazing, if you ask me."

"No one asked you," Iletus said. "You were given an instruction. That is all you need to know. Kill him."

I shook my head.

"The choice is between you and him," Galen said. "You must understand that."

"I understand that is your choice, what you want," I said. "I don't have anything to do with that. I'm making this choice, not to kill him."

Galen's stare bore into mine for a long time, scowling. I held his eyes, expecting him to draw his own sword and kill me.

So be it. I couldn't save humans by killing one. I would only become the murderer myself.

Galen placed his hand on the hilt of his sword. I stood straight.

Galen shook his head and spoke to Iletus. "Bind them both and take them below. Place them in separate rooms. We will sort this out back at the Citadel."

Chapter 19

The Power of Choice

Galen summoned me that evening.

We had sailed back from Katara Isle. I spent the time alone, bound, and in silence. Arriving back at the Citadel, they removed the ropes and sequestered me to my room for a few hours, where more salves and oils waited. I used them, changed into new clothes, and rested, waiting.

Waiting has always been torture for me. As a teen, it was worse. So when Lyne arrived to take me to meet with Galen, I bounded up from my bed, despite the dull pains over my body, and went along. No matter what Galen decided, it was better than waiting.

Halfway up the tower to Galen's study, I rethought my eagerness. My legs and ribs yelled at me the whole way. I made it to the top of the tower, Lyne quiet beside me, and stood before the door with the Citadel emblem mounted on the wood, the golden eagle with swords as wings. Lyne left me there.

I hadn't even knocked when Galen's voice called from within. "Enter."

Turning the latch on the door, I pushed it open and moved inside.

Galen sat at the same desk, although this time he stared at me, his hands in his lap. He gestured to a chair. "Sit."

I strode over to the chair and settled within it.

"I am deciding if I should kill you now," Galen said. "This is your chance to convince me to live."

"And Franz?"

"I must also determine what to do with him."

My stomach tightened. "Another test?"

Galen's lips became a line. "As I said before, everything is a test, an opportunity for us to see who you are and who you will become."

"I understand."

The elf's eyes narrowed. "I'm not sure you do. You are human, and for many of the elves in the Citadel here, it was folly to even bring you here, much less to teach or train you. It is utter insanity for some to consider sending you back to your homeland with that training. I gave you a command, and you refused. You have no value to us if we cannot trust you."

I nodded. "Just so we're clear, I wouldn't kill a defenseless boy."

"You will have to kill people as a Bladeguard."

"In battle, sure," I said.

"You believe your future is one of battle alone? We assassinate and work in the shadows more than any ever see."

My jaw tightened. "What happened today wasn't an assassination. It was an execution."

Galen waved a hand. "The command doesn't matter. Only obedience."

"You're saying you have the power to tell me to do anything you wish, and I have to comply? Despite what is right and wrong?"

"You're not the one to determine what is best for the Empire, what is right and wrong." Galen shifted his weight. "That is for other, better beings, people who have lived for a thousand years. You've lived, what, fourteen years? And you believe you understand the complexities and complications to run an Empire?"

I shook my head. "Not at all. I wouldn't try to run an Empire even if I could."

"And yet you still refused my command? That was a central test, and you failed."

I sniffed. "I disagree."

Galen blinked. "Explain."

"If you say I failed according to your standards, then yes, that's true. But my concern wasn't for you or the Empire or Iletus or whoever. I was concerned with something more important."

Galen raised a brow. "And what was that concern?"

"My soul." I leaned forward. "You see, I believe that I possess a soul, something that is mine and mine alone, a part of me that matters more than anything else, and I'm responsible for what I do with that soul. You may have the power to kill me based on what is good for the Empire, but you don't have an authority that trumps mine when it comes to my soul."

"Even at your own peril and death? At the cost of your life?"

"Right. Again, that is my choice, to die rather than give up my soul. In that, according to a different measure, I was successful."

Galen groaned and shook his head. "You cannot be trained as a Bladeguard, then. We must find another."

"I also disagree with that."

Galen frowned. "How so?"

"You had me read Contigus before, one of the first tests, and when Lyne asked for something for me to read, you sent that book down."

The elf hesitated. "Continue."

"Contigus has an essay called *The Sacred Soul*. I read it the other day. You're familiar with it?"

Galen nodded.

"I really liked it. If you remember, he argues that if a person – elf or human or dwarf or whoever – complies based on fear or threat, then no one can trust that person. That person has no internal compass and is ... unpredictable. You have to always be on your guard around them, watching, because it is threat and fear that cause obedience."

Galen shifted in his chair.

"But someone who acts according to the value of his or her own soul, however, will do what they believe is right no matter the consequences," I said. "That person complies according to their own choice, and they refuse according to their own conscience. That is the person you can trust. That is the person to give more power and authority to." I shrugged. "At least, that was what he said in that essay."

"Fascinating." Galen sat back in his chair. "And while I'm surprised at your resourcefulness and respect the argument, Contigus was an idealist. The kingdom became corrupt, those elves with a supposed soul, the ones he said to infuse with more power, abused that authority and our nation suffered for many centuries. This is a different time, one he did not have the privilege of seeing."

I nodded. "Then you do what you think you have to. That is your decision. I made mine."

I used the arguments from Contigus and his essay, true. However, I had been surprised how similar that elven philosopher's thoughts aligned with the scriptures of El. I might not have been brave enough to tell him then or admit it, but I sounded much like my uncle when I spoke to Galen. I sounded like the Prophet, dressed in an elven idealist.

Galen's face went blank, and he stared at me for several minutes.

"You've given me much to consider," Galen said at last. "Return to your room. We will talk tomorrow."

I rose from the chair and exited the room.

I got to live another evening, at least.

Chapter 20

The Greatest Slavery

No one waited for me when I left Galen's study, not even Lyne, and I began the long descent.

Climbing the stairs had been painful, but stepping down one after another grated on my knee and the sore muscles of my leg. I passed one level and then the next, hallways and rooms toward the center of the tower. The windows on my left gave a view to the clear sky pinpricked with hundreds of stars, the three moons off over the horizon.

I gritted my teeth against the aches. When I breathed deeper, my ribs started pricking me, as well.

I had to focus on each step in the dim evening light, regular oil lamps in golden housings along the wall giving warm glows, but much remained in shadow. I used the tiny bed in the small room far below the Citadel as a reward.

My mind was so preoccupied that I didn't see the figure launching from a doorway to my right until something metal reflected the low lamplight from the wall behind me.

I slung my body to the side starting with my shoulder, which threw the rest of me off balance, and I stepped back to recover, tripping on a stair and tumbling backwards.

The tumble was lucky, because the knife coming toward me would have stuck straight in the middle of my chest but instead sliced across the bicep of my left arm. The cut stung cold while I continued to fall and landed the stairs, corners slamming into my side.

He stood over me, his height imposing there in the dim stairway.

"Franz!" I reached over and put a hand on the cut on my arm, blood beginning to seep into my palm.

Franz hunched his shoulders, the knife in his hand ready to strike, his teeth bared.

I lifted a bloody hand to stay him. "Wait. Just wait. You don't have to do this."

"Only one of us will survive. You or me. This is the only way." He lunged with the blade at my midsection. I scrambled and slid over and away, suffering only a minor cut along the outside of my thigh.

While I scrambled further and he gathered to attack, I said, "No. That's what they want you to think."

Franz leapt at me, and I rolled over to the left. He landed and leaned forward, stretching out to cut me, ripping at my tunic but missing my skin.

"You think you're so smart." He got to his feet, facing me. "But you're a gedder idiot."

I made my way to my feet, retreating, aching muscles now joined by the slice on my arm. "Maybe, but think about it." I moved a couple more steps away. "The elves have been doing this for centuries, dividing, getting us to see each other as enemies. We can be different."

Franz scoffed and paused. "Don't you see where we are? Who we're up against? They make the rules."

I thought of my father, my mother, Reyan and Kendra, their belief in a god that taught something different. "No, they don't. Or they don't have to."

He growled and chased me the, punching with a fist that flew past my head. Now the oil lamp was behind him, and shadows covered his face. "Shut up!"

I dodged another swipe of the knife, backing away. Franz was bigger, stronger, and added with my injuries, I really would be a gedder idiot if I tried to fight him.

"There has to be another way," I said. "A way we don't have to die."

His eyes narrowed, his voice low. "There's not."

He rushed me, incredibly fast, both hands attacking at once, and while I attempted to avoid him, I stumbled, my legs weak. His fist caught my jaw, snapping my head to the side. He aimed the blade at my chest. I twisted and brought a leg up in desperation, and the knife plunged deep into the meat of my thigh.

I cried out in pain and swung my elbow wide, trying to get him off, and I struck him in the temple. He staggered and stood straight, trying to stay upright, leaving the knife in my leg.

In my exhaustion and agony and within a tick of time, I glanced at my bloody hands and the knife sticking out. The frustration of centuries of elven oppression and Franz refusing to listen and the Bladeguard putting us in this position, boys who should be brothers fighting each other, all of it fueled an anger that overwhelmed me.

The rage ruled me.

With wide eyes and yelling at the top of my lungs, I yanked the knife from my leg and tossed it at him in one motion. The knife turned end over end and sank into Franz's collarbone. He threw his head back and screamed.

There was no pause or thought when I rose and leapt from the stairs. Lifting my legs, I rammed my knees into his solar plexus. The breath left him in a whoosh, his eyes bulged, mouth a circle, and his arms whipped around as his body sailed through the air.

Since the stairway curved up and down the outside of the tower, he flew toward the wall ... and the glass oil lamp in a golden housing.

He hit the wall and lamp with the back of his head and shoulders, glass shattering and metal wrenching. The next heartbeat, flames engulfed his hair and the top of his tunic. He began another scream, this time one of terror and torture, and he gyrated before he fell on his side in an awkward position on the stairs. Something in his body crunched.

Franz bounced, continuing to thrash about, his arms and hands smacking his head and shoulders, trying to put out the flames.

I collapsed to my knees, instinctively reaching out a hand like I could help him. But I had caused it.

He was beyond my help, mitres away, rolling and plummeting down the stairs, more wet and cracking sounds punctuating the constant cackle of flame and his scream that seemed to take an impossible amount of time.

One more popping sound, like a broken bone, and he stopped screeching. He flopped to a halt, burning but laying still, his head off at an odd angle.

I groaned like I'd been punched and leaned over, sitting.

Footfalls sounded on the stairs from behind. They landed beside me, and I glanced up, knowing who it was before I saw his face.

"I ... tried to stop him," I said.

Galen raised a brow at me and then regarded the body burning on the stairs below us. "I would say you succeeded."

But that wasn't what I meant.

I lay in the bed in my room, Lyne next to me on a stool. Under the meager candlelight, she expertly stitched the cut across my bicep. She had already tended to the wound on my thigh.

Up in the tower, slaves had doused Franz's body, and they carried me down the stairs, through the Citadel and into the slave quarters, placing me on my bed. Lyne had arrived a few minutes later.

I gazed up at the ceiling. "He wouldn't listen."

"Hmmm." Lyne continued to weave the stitching.

"I told him we didn't have to do it, that we didn't have to fight. But he wouldn't hear it."

Lyne didn't respond for a few moments. She glanced down at the eagle tattoo on her wrist. "I have been a slave my whole life. The greatest slavery is the one of the mind and heart. He was bound in his thoughts and emotions. That is the most difficult place to be free, from the soul. Even many who live in palaces, they may wear no chains but are still bound from within."

The image of the Cursed came to mind, a horror within the ruins of a palace.

"You believe in the soul?"

"They tell me I'm not allowed to believe in the soul." But when she said it, she smiled.

Only a few hours ago, I had argued for my own soul.

I breathed in and out, almost relishing the pain in my ribs, as if I deserved it.

"I – I killed him."

"Yes," she said. "But it is what he chose."

I wasn't so sure, but I understood her meaning. That was the path he chose, and I reacted in anger and wrath. A part of me emerged a killer. I was scared for my soul.

I looked at her then, the candlelight throwing waves of yellow across her face. My vision blurred with tears. "I never killed anyone before."

She kept her attention on the needle in her hand. "If you are to be trained here among the elves, it will be but the first of many."

I snorted and peered back up at the ceiling. "Lyne?"

"Yes, Caleb."

"What's the date today?"

She looked up. "The date?"

"The day, the month."

Lyne sighed. "The thirteenth of the month of Yol."

"Thank you," I said. "That's what I thought."

"Why do you ask?"

I cleared my throat. "Today is my nameday. I'm fifteen years."

Lyne sat motionless for a few seconds. "Well, happy nameday, Caleb."

For my fifteenth nameday, I had killed someone. She was right. It was only the first of many.

Happy nameday to me.

Chapter 21

This is How it Began

Two days passed before Galen summoned me once more.

Lyne had continued to tend to my wounds, checking on me and bringing me food. I began walking and moving around the next day, but she chided me, threatening me if I pulled her stitches.

I read more essays from Contigus while I rested, however my mind stayed busy, Franz and Mande and my family dominating my thoughts.

And my father and those parchments the Prophet copied, meticulously, gently, documents from the divine that spoke of the value of a soul.

Lyne gave me a crutch to climb the stairs around the tower to Galen's study, which I didn't think I needed but made me glad the more I ascended. When I passed the area where Franz and I had fought and he died, halfway up the tower, the area had been cleaned and a new lamp fixture in place of the broken one. No sign of the violence or death that had taken place.

I made the trek alone this time, and I rapped my knuckles on the door, the golden eagle with blades for feathers on its wings stared back at me.

"Enter," Galen said.

Walking into the room, Galen reposed at his desk, and Iletus sat next to him. Galen held the staff I found on Katara Isle across his lap. He waved at a chair across from them. I sat.

Galen peered down at the white pole and then back at me. "Many have been to that cursed island over thousands of years.

Perhaps one of them found that cavern before and didn't survive, or they survived and took other treasure that has been lost to time, as their stories have. In my lifetime, however, you're the only one to have found that underground place and lived to speak of it. Do you know what it is you discovered?"

"That dragons were real? More than legend?"

Galen nodded. "That is significant, yes. It does not mean all the legends are true, but we can be sure now that they did exist. And if those creatures, then others, too. But it means something more."

I raised my brow, waiting. Galen gestured at Iletus.

"We knew Jeromus as a wizard that perverted and abused his power, as we explained," Iletus said. "What was a mystery to us was exactly the process he attempted. Now we know. He possessed the remains of a dragon. A skull."

After a couple moments, I glanced between them. "Yeah? So?"

Iletus continued. "Dragons were powerful, some say divine. Divinity is easily attributed to beings so massive and mysterious along with the distance of history allowing for embellishments and creative retellings. However, legends spring from a seed of truth, and if we are to believe at least the seed, then we know the ancient wizards killed dragons to extract some amount of power from them in an attempt to become ... immortal. This happened at great cost, as we now understand."

"You think that's what Jeromus did," I said. "But even the bones?"

Iletus nodded. "Yes. His own hubris cursed him. The presence of the dragon skull is what keeps him tied to the island. He must stay within proximity to stay alive."

"Dragon bones are as strong as Kryan steel." Galen lifted the staff from his lap. "As a material, it cannot be forged, it must be carved, and we don't know any metal strong enough to cut or break dragonbone, not to mention that besides the cavern you discovered, we don't know where any dragonbone exists today. That makes this weapon unique, indeed."

I inclined my head. "You think that's a weapon?"

"A weapon or a symbol of power or both," Iletus said. "The point is that your discovery on the island gave us more insight into many mysteries, notably the root of Jeromus's curse."

"Great." I raised and lowered a shoulder. "Is that why you called me here?"

"Part of it," Galen said. "The discovery of the dragon skull on the island combined with your survival of the various tests over the past couple days, it has all impressed us."

Iletus shifted in his seat. "Yet your refusal to kill Franz when commanded is a mark against you, and a significant one."

"To train a human as a Bladeguard is dangerous, for you and for Iletus and myself," Galen said. "There will be a host of elves praying to the nine gods, hoping for this to fail, looking for any reason to kill that human."

"And working to kill the elves that gave a human the opportunity to become one of the greatest warriors in the world." Iletus frowned.

Galen nodded. "We have spent the last two days considering and discussing your fate."

The room fell silent, both elves silent and motionless, staring at me. My fate. Kill me and search for another? Give me the opportunity to be a Bladeguard to betray humanity?

I tensed, my fingers gripping the arms of the chair. "And?"

Galen blinked and leaned forward. "While Iletus still maintains some protest, we have agreed that you will begin training with the other initiates."

I relaxed, blowing out a breath.

"This is no favor to you, Caleb," Galen said. "The training ahead of you is the most physically difficult warrior instruction in the world. And you will be at a disadvantage, since the other initiates will be actively against your success in this endeavor."

"You will also begin in a probationary period." Iletus squared his shoulders. "The Master and I will not announce this probation to the others, as you will already have great resistance among the other masters and trainees. But we will be watching."

"Because of these reasons," Galen said, "and our conversation the other day, this must be your choice."

My eyes narrowed. "My choice?"

Galen took a deep breath. "Yes, you must choose for yourself. Will you agree and commit to the Bladeguard training, knowing all it entails and our expectation that you obey what we command?"

I scoffed. "Or die, right? That's the choice?"

"That has always been the reality," Galen said. "Yes. Death … or a continued life of pain and unimaginable hardship."

I scowled, averting my eyes, not answering.

Galen leaned back in his chair. "Have you ever seen a sword forged, Caleb?"

Not looking up, I shook my head.

"The greatest blades take time," Galen said. "Under great heat and fire, the metal must first be purged of all impurities, then it becomes malleable. With the right material, the maker then begins to pound and shape the metal, over and over, with more heat and patience and abuse. But all that violence has a purpose. A blade strong and sharp enough to endure. And to kill. Do you understand?"

The Blade of El. The prophecy of the *Brendel*. Did Galen know those old scriptures? Was he aware how much he sounded like the illegal scrolls of El? Or was it a coincidence?

I couldn't ask him without giving away too much and placing my sister and family in danger. "You want me to be a weapon?"

"We will forge you to be a weapon," Galen said. "You will emerge the greatest masterpiece of my life, able to kill any and all who oppose you."

I hesitated. "Even you?"

Iletus flashed his eyes at Galen, and the Master of the Citadel stared back at me with a blank expression for ticks of time that stretched too long.

Then Galen smirked. "Anything is possible."

Iletus shook his head.

"What is your choice, then?" Galen's mouth now became a line.

Galen and Iletus challenged me with the physical hardship and anguish of the Bladeguard training. Whether they did so to encourage or discourage me, I didn't know. These elves played games, more than implied among the resistance of other initiates and elven instructors they mentioned. I didn't doubt the physical demands would be near impossible.

But that wasn't the greatest challenge for me.

They would educate me, train me, make me a weapon of body and mind, a great power, much like trying to use the dragon bones to become immortal. But that was the way of pride, and the result was a curse. In the course of training, they would do all they could to take my soul.

The first essay Galen had me read by Contigus gave severe warning considering the danger of becoming the evil we fight. In the search to do good, we begin to justify evil and become the villain of our own story.

That would be my true challenge. If I lost my soul along the way and became like them, thought and acted and believed like them, then it would be better to die, to refuse and end it with my soul intact.

As my parents had taught me, passed on in a memory that always haunted me of a cave and my mother's screams in my ear. I would not dishonor my father and mother by losing that which made me human.

The question I faced was this – Caleb, will you commit to training among your enemies while fighting to retain your soul? Will you fight evil without becoming a villain? Will you accept that challenge?

I raised my eyes and sat straight in the chair. I met their stares.

"Yes."

Another few moments passed, the weight of that one word giving each of us pause.

"Very well," Galen said. "You start tomorrow."

And that was how it began.

End of Book 1

Acknowledgements:

To my wife, Becca, who continues to support and believe in me.

To my children who are becoming excellent writers who give me honest feedback.

To God for all his gifts and blessings that made this possible.

Links:

If you enjoyed this novella, you can read more in the world of Eres with *The LIVING STONE, The BLADES OF WAR,* and *The FIRE REBORN.*

And check out the new book, *SHIELD OF THE KING: ELOWEN BOOK ONE.*

Also subscribe to my YouTube Channel – Great Stories Changed the World

Go to www.mbmooney.com for more information.

Thank you!

Author's Note:

More extras! Here is an excerpt from the epic fantasy *THE LIVING STONE*!!

Chapter 1

Home Again

Caleb De'Ador's steel gray eyes squinted against the late afternoon sun while the boat beneath him docked in the harbor of Asya, the largest city on the continent of humanity. The elven kingdom of Kryus from across the ocean ruled and oppressed this land where Caleb had been raised until leaving years ago.

He returned today to the place of his birth. And where he would likely meet his end.

The *Far Lover* – a sleek elven vessel constructed with black Liorian wood – came to rest at the end of a busy pier, and Caleb stood at the bow. He turned his bearded face from the wind to watch the human workers secure the craft to the moorings, his shoulder length brown hair falling across his eyes. The shirtless and barefoot men each bore a small eagle tattoo on their left wrist that marked them as corporate slaves.

Caleb had paid for his passage back in Kaltiel but slept in the hold with the slaves, making no friends among the elven bosses on the long voyage across the ocean from Kryus. He wanted to say his farewells to the slaves as he left the boat, but he decided to satisfy himself with one nearby – Dun.

He had spent the most time with Dun along the journey. A gregarious man, Dun was hardened but quick with a joke; his hearty laugh was good company, especially over a game of Tablets. When Caleb shared ancient stories of heroic men and women, Dun listened but dismissed the tales as wave whispers. He did ask to hear more, however, almost every night. Caleb did his best to remember the stories of the ancient scriptures, tales told by his father and his Uncle Reyan years ago.

Caleb now approached Dun, and the man lowered his eyes and hunched his shoulders up on deck in sight of the elven Captain driving the men to their work. Caleb stretched out his hand. Dun took it in friendship.

"Remember to keep your ear to the wind, my friend," Caleb said. "And do not be surprised if you hear that things are beginning to change."

Dun gave a smile missing a couple teeth. "I will. Well met."

"Well met," Caleb said.

The momentary pause in activity caught the Captain's attention, and he hurried in their direction. Caleb adjusted the backpack on his shoulder and left Dun to his work.

The Captain was average height for an elf – a head shorter than the common man – with cropped blond hair and sharp pointed ears. He wore a plain, long white robe and leather sandals, and he walked with a slight limp, which he proudly claimed to have acquired in the War of Accession. Caleb was skeptical, however. Elves possessed long lives and aggrandized memories.

When they passed each other, the Captain turned and shot Caleb a glare. After centuries of Kryan control, humans learned to bow to the elves. But Caleb didn't avert his stare. He stood straight, reaching over with his hand to hold the leather bracer that covered his left forearm. The elf frowned while Caleb held the gaze.

The Captain broke away first and spun, cursing and yelling at the men moving quickly about the ship, a nine-thonged whip held in his right hand. Caleb began to move to the plank that led off the boat. He peeked from the corner of his eye; the elven Captain rushed Dun.

"Come on, you piece of crit! We haven't got all breakin' day!"

Dun simply nodded, bowing to the Captain and staring down, pulling a line with all his might to furl the massive white sail.

The Captain took another two steps and raised the whip, bringing it down upon Dun's bare back. The man tied off the line and knelt in a huddle, his arms crossing to protect his head. The Captain continued to whip him.

Caleb froze two paces away from the walkway off the ship. He rolled his shoulders while the scars on his own back from an elven whip began to itch beneath his white shirt, the cloak, and the burden of the canvas pack. His fists clenched at his side in the midst of the man's cries of agony.

"Break me," Caleb whispered.

Spinning around, he faced the Captain and Dun.

The Captain continued to beat Dun, blood dripping from several rips on the man's flesh and onto the deck. The rest of the human crew slowed in their work, their faces blank. Dun yelled in pain through gritted teeth. The Captain began to grin.

Caleb sprinted, his feet quiet across the deck, and he stopped in a crouch in the small space between Dun and the Captain. The Captain brought down the whip, but this time Caleb caught the leather thongs on his covered left forearm. The thin lashes wound around his wrist with a snapping sound. He reached out and grabbed the whip with his left hand.

The Captain stood rigid. Dun groaned and caught his breath, collapsing to the deck.

Sneering at the elf, Caleb pulled on the whip. The Captain held fast to the handle and was drawn into a right-handed strike between the eyes, his head snapping back. Gasping while he faltered, the Captain stumbled, and Caleb yanked the whip away, standing from the crouched position and rotating into a flying right kick across the side of the Captain's head.

The Captain's legs buckled, and he dropped to the deck in an unconscious heap.

The human crew froze, watching him with fear in their eyes. Caleb unwound the whip from his forearm and threw it overboard. He heard yelling from down below in the hold, the First Mate preparing the cargo to be unloaded. "What's going on up there?"

Time to go, Caleb thought.

He adjusted his pack, nodded to Dun and the rest of the slaves, and walked towards the plank leading to the quay.

As Caleb stepped on the pier and strode away from the ship, the First Mate screamed, "Hey – what the shog?"

Caleb reached back and pulled the hood of his cloak over his head, moving quickly – without looking desperate – down the pier towards the bustling docks north of the white city walls.

The cacophony of sounds in the harbor surrounded him: loud voices, profanity, wooden crates shifting, horses pulling wagons. The scent of dung and sweat caught his nostrils. Many humans also wore the eagle tattoo on their left wrist.

At the end of the pier, Caleb swung right and inclined his head enough to see the First Mate of the *Far Lover* pushing through the crowd and following him, calling angrily with a short sword in his hand. Caleb cursed and maneuvered through the throng of people and cargo toward the wide gate into the city.

Two elven Cityguard stood at the gate, clothed in their gray tunics, light steel armor and helmets, the elven gladi – short swords – at their side. The guard, engrossed in their conversation, didn't even look at him when he passed through the wide opening in the wall.

Caleb knew the First Mate followed him, however, so he pressed into the northern quarter of Asya. Old, dilapidated warehouses rose on either side, human workers busy while elven supervisors stood over them. After two blocks, he stole a glance behind him, and two steel Cityguard helmets bobbed in his direction. He took a deep breath and ran.

Leaving the warehouses, he found himself among tenements, gray rectangular buildings that had once been painted bright colors. Kryus had burned all of Asya while conquering the ancient city, and they rebuilt it to show their compassion. That was centuries ago. The paint and color had faded to nothing. Odors of human waste and decay overpowered Caleb, nauseated him. The few hollow-eyed and bone thin humans in the streets were clothed in rags.

Turning left down a side alley between two tenements, he glanced over his shoulder. The two Cityguard gained on him, five mitres away. The First Mate had gone.

The alley narrowed along the length of the tenements, littered with debris, and beyond the shadows, Caleb peered ahead. A dead end. He slowed to a stop, sighing, and he whirled to see the Cityguard jogging towards him. The two guard completely blocked the way in the narrow alley, their gladi in their hands.

Caleb let his pack drop to the floor, and he kicked it to the side. He removed his cloak, his eyes never leaving the Cityguard in their approach, and he draped the mantle over his pack. He stepped forward and stood with his hands relaxed at his side.

The two elves halted two mitres away. They caught their breath, both scowling. "You need to come with us," the first Cityguard said.

The sight of the guard triggered a distinct childhood memory – holding his weeping baby sister in his arms in a dark cave, hearing the distant screams of his mother as the Cityguard did things to her that he could only guess, an imagination that had become more detailed as he grew into manhood.

There was a letter in his pack, and gold, but he dismissed that option. With his mother's screams in his head, he sneered back at the guard. He angled his body with his left foot slightly forward, his knees bent, his feet shoulder width apart.

The two elves hesitated, blinking and sharing a glance in surprise when they saw his eyes. Their frowns deepened at his gall. Trained to work as a team, the two guard tread forward with their gladi before them. Their faces were intent on their prey, sobered in their duty.

Caleb had been trained, as well, and by better masters. The Cityguard on his right stabbed forward, and Caleb leapt backward out of range of the gladus. The elf on the left immediately struck out with his sword behind his partner's move, and this time Caleb slid to his left, stretched out with his right hand and grabbed the sword arm of the elf. He lashed out with his left hand and crushed the Cityguard's windpipe.

The Cityguard gurgled, trying to gasp, and Caleb spun the elf towards his partner, using the wounded one as a shield and pushing both guard back against the wall of the alley.

The second guard's gladus caught between himself and his partner, and he struggled to free it while Caleb twisted the wounded elf's right wrist. He heard a popping sound as the sword fell to the dirt of the alley.

Caleb let the suffocating elf fall while he jumped straight up and brought his elbow down into the face of the second Cityguard. The elf sputtered when blood spouted from his nose, and Caleb wasted no time in crossing his arms and grabbing the elf by the neck. The elf blindly swung his gladus and slashed across Caleb's right forearm. In one fluid and violent motion, Caleb turned and threw the elf over his shoulder against the opposite wall of the alley. The elf's spine broke, the elf dead before he hit the dirt.

The elf at Caleb's feet still clutched at his neck, straining for breath, for life. Caleb stepped over him. Walking over to his pack, he opened it and picked out a new shirt. He tore the one he wore off his body, ripped it into a few strips and dressed the gash on his forearm. It wasn't deep but bled heavily. He tugged the new shirt on, placed the cloak into the pack, and he slung the backpack over his shoulders.

Both elves were dead by the time Caleb exited the shadows of the alley and turned left onto the main street, glancing both ways to make sure there weren't any more threats.

There were none. But the First Mate might have gone for help, and when the Captain returned to consciousness, the elves of the city would be looking for him.

He would need somewhere to hide tonight, but it had been more than seventeen years since he was last in this city with his uncle. A lifetime ago.

He could only think of one place. He hoped he could find it.

—

Crossing the city, Caleb used as many side streets as he could. The sun fell behind the city wall, the western horizon changing to shades of orange and red.

He paused in front of an apartment building closer to the Merchant District on the southern edge of Asya and stopped a young man on the street, a thin youth with bushy dark hair, pallid skin, and dilated pupils. Caleb could smell the sickly sweet scent of Sorcos on the young man deep in the thrall of the drug.

"Excuse me," Caleb said. "Do the Re'Wyl's live in this building?"

"Whu?" The youth's body swayed when his head turned to look at Caleb.

The Kryan Empire generously provided Sorcos, a drug they claimed entertained the mind and healed the body. What medicinal effects it had, Caleb had never seen, but it was highly addictive and produced a tranquil and somnolent population.

Many humans in the Kryan Empire went hungry. But they could always find Sorcos.

Caleb spoke louder now that he had the boy's attention. "Jyson and Rose Re'Wyl. Do they still live here?" He pointed to the apartment building.

"Oh, yeah. Up on third be the rooms o' Jyson; rooms three-four." He pursed his lips in satisfaction.

"Thank you." Caleb walked into the building. After he climbed the narrow stairwell up to the third floor, he had trouble making out the numbers in the dim hallway. He found the fourth door, on the corner of the building, and he knocked. The door opened.

Rose had always been a handsome woman, and while she was now older, that hadn't changed. She wore a baggy red tunic over a brown pleated skirt.

Running a hand through her graying blond hair, she smiled at him without recognition. "May I help you?"

"Rose. It's me. Caleb De'Ador."

It took her a moment to register the name, but once she did, her eyes widened. She froze, and her face tightened. "Caleb? What – what are you doing here?"

A man's voice echoed from within the apartment. "Who is it?"

Caught between her husband and the man at her door, Rose hesitated, but after a moment searching his eyes, she grabbed Caleb's arm, the one with the fresh wound. He winced as she pulled him into the room. "Come in, quickly." She shut the door behind him.

The main room was small and sparse but functional. A small table with four chairs stood in the corner next to a wood stove and there were cabinets on the wall. A short couch and two ragged but inviting cushioned reading chairs sat on the opposite side of the room. Books and parchments were piled on the floor.

A man with wavy white hair and a full white beard regarded Caleb from one of the chairs. He stood.

Jyson was fit for his age, and he wore a simple crimson tunic over brown pants.

Rose hovered next to Caleb and faced her husband. "Jy, he says he's Caleb De'Ador."

Jyson frowned. "That boy disappeared more than fifteen years ago."

"Yes, I know. But I'm back now," Caleb said.

"He has the same eyes." Rose's voice was low.

"We'll need more than a likeness of the eyes to believe a man is someone we thought long dead." Jyson's glare challenged him.

They want proof? Caleb thought. *Very well.*

"My name is Caleb De'Ador. My uncle is Reyan Be'Luthel, also known by many in Erelon as the Prophet. He is an enemy of Kryus for traveling to nations, cities, and towns and preaching the truth of El, the Creator, truth that the Empire has tried for centuries to suppress or eradicate. He teaches men that they were created to be free. After the Kryan Empire burned my parents at the stake, my little sister and I lived and traveled with the Prophet and his family. I was last here seventeen years ago. I was thirteen years old, and my sister and I slept on that floor with your two kids."

Both of them froze. Two long, quiet heartbeats passed.

"Only a handful of people could know that, Jy," Rose said. "Only a handful in the world."

Jyson's jaw clenched. "What happened to you?"

Caleb took a deep breath. "I was … kidnapped by the Kryan Empire while we were in the city of Landen sixteen years ago. I am back."

"You escaped?" Jyson asked.

"Not exactly. I was being trained by the elves, and my Master sent me away once I was ready."

Jyson's lip curled. "You work for the elves?"

"No. I am free and here on my own." Caleb held up his arm, rolled back the sleeve of the shirt and showed them the bloody cloth around the gash. "I just had a run-in with the Cityguard in the slave quarter. I need medical attention and a place to stay the night, maybe some help buying a horse and supplies. I will be gone first thing in the morning. I can't stay here long. They'll be looking for me."

Jyson shook his head in disbelief.

Rose finally sniffed and gently took Caleb's left hand. "Come to the table. At least I can clean that up for you. Would you like some tea?"

"Thank you," he said.

She led him to the table. He dropped his pack nearby and sat in one of the wooden chairs. He was soon sipping hot bitter tea while Rose took a bowl of water and a clean rag and washed out the cut on his forearm. She wrapped it again in dry cloth.

Jyson continued to glare at him from across the room, but he eventually walked over to the table and joined them. Rose set a cup of tea in front of him.

"Speaking of my Uncle," Caleb said. "When was the last you heard from him?"

Rose faltered, hesitating before she finished tying off the cloth around the wound, and then she sat next to him, pouring herself some tea. Jyson sighed and rubbed his beard, his eyes flicking to his wife. Rose blinked slowly.

"How long you been in the city?" Jyson asked.

Caleb looked from Rose back to Jyson. "Just got off the boat this afternoon."

"He don't know, Jy," Rose said.

"What don't I know?"

Jyson leaned forward over the small table. "Caleb, my boy, your Uncle Reyan's been captured and imprisoned by the Empire. They brought him here to the prison. He's at the Pyts."

—+—

The Dark Gate was concealed within the Kaleti Mountains, peaks that spread across the southwest region of the great continent of Ereland, also known as the land of humanity on the world of Eres.

Thoros the Demilord stood in the darkness within the mountain, waiting for the Gate to open. A weak red glow from the deep fiery caverns below was the only light, although his black eyes could see clearly. The scorching heat of the Underland wafted from behind him.

Known as the *Mahsaksa'ar* in the First Tongue, the Dark Gate was a half-circle of black stone, smooth and unnatural, and it was one of two portals to the Underland, or the *Heol Ra'eres*. The Gate was twenty mitres tall and ten wide.

The Gate shuddered when it split, opening with a deafening sound, the gray stone doors swinging wide, scraping and groaning. Thoros rolled his muscular shoulders and stepped out from the Underland into the world above.

Storms raged upon the mountain and the surrounding region, the three moons of Eres coming into alignment – the green moon of Cynadi and the blue of Motali eclipsed by the red moon of Vysti – and wreaking havoc upon the land. Black clouds gathered, tornadoes ripped through the foothills, and rain and hail laid waste to the countryside. Thick lightning accompanied by deafening thunder dug small craters into Maed and the plains to the north. The mountain trembled.

Thoros twisted at his waist to peer up at the apex of the Gate. Written upon it was a script in a language older than even the First Tongue. Some once called it prophecy, others a curse, but more accurately it was a command from the Creator, the one responsible for its construction and the imprisonment of the demics into the Underland.

The command inscribed in melted blood gems stated that every 527 years, when the three moons of Eres fell into alignment in their orbit over the mountain of Maed, the Gate would open and allow a force of demics and one Demilord back into the world.

The script placed the responsibility of defeating those monsters into the hands of ancient human warriors.

The Demilord stood two and a half mitres tall. His dark red skin, hairless and thick as armor, had curses etched in black ink over his bare muscular torso and thick arms, each painful stroke a reminder of the dark power of the Underland; every excruciating phrase in his flesh had been earned as a reward from his Master. He wore a simple pair of loose black trousers that hung down below his knees. His eyes shone black and beady beneath a prominent forehead, and two large black horns curved up and outward from his temples to face forward. Two ebony tusks protruded from the bottom row of sharpened teeth in his mouth. He had pointed ears and a small nose. His hands and feet were three-fingered claws with long black talons at the end.

Thoros stood strong and immovable as the storm and gales beat at him. He took a breath of air, cold in contrast to the dark halls and caverns of the Underland, and his body adjusted to the chill. The night was bright, almost blinding compared to the black caverns, and he surveyed the northern vista from the face of Maed.

He called his army of demics forth.

The common demics issued forth from the Dark Gate behind him in droves, a handful of them holding clubs fashioned from the stalagmites of the deep caves of the Underland. Most were weaponless; their talons and tusks would tear through any surface short of iron and steel.

The demics looked much like Thoros but a third of his size and more simian with longer arms and shorter legs. The impish creatures poured past Thoros, screaming in pain, a high pitched screeching sound, when the clean water and hail hit their red flesh, skin that had been scarred and tempered by the heat and dryness of the Underland.

The demics were not capable of much thought beyond destruction, hunger, anger and fear. Thoros commanded them with a telepathic link to continue through the Gate until as many demics as possible could make it. His orders were filled with implied threat in the face of the anguish from the hail and rain. They were created to obey, and he designed to drive them.

He also promised them they would feed on the flesh of the living races. That helped to overcome their fear.

The precipitation caused Thoros pain, as well, but his hide withstood it. The moon of Cynadi moved into the eastern sky and Vysti to the south. The storms lowered their intensity but still continued.

When the Gate finally closed, one demic was not quite fast enough, and the stone closed upon him and crushed the creature, black blood splattering on the stony ground. Other demics ran headlong into the shut barrier inside the mountain. Thoros could sense them in his mind. How many had made it through? Thoros guessed at least eight, perhaps, ten thousand.

Bana Sahat, the Lord of the Underland, had bred, trained, and tortured the Demilord for a millennium to come to the world of Eres and lead the demic horde for a single purpose: to find the Key that would permanently free the perverse monsters from the dark and fiery prison of the Underland.

The Lord of the Underland and the demics once lived in the world above, thousands of years ago, ruling the night and feeding on the flesh of the First Ones. But Yosu and the warriors of El had driven the demics back after many years of war, banishing them into the deep chambers of the Underland where they starved or ate one another instead of the delicious flesh of human, elf, or dwarf. While the sun and rain tortured them, at least here they would feed.

The demics were ravenous. So was Thoros, but he ate something far different and more powerful.

The same telepathic link that allowed him to communicate with the demics also helped him to locate the Key, the *Heol-caeg*. Thoros closed his black eyes and took a deep breath. North. Due north.

This was his hour, his time to do what none of the other fourteen Demilords before him could accomplish. He would teach the humans of this age the meaning of evil and hate and set his race free again to rule the night.

He opened his eyes again, and a smile spread on his face.

Thoros ran behind the demics, driving them north with an audible and mental roar, a demand to find the Key, and destroy and consume every living thing in their path.

Continue reading! Purchase *The LIVING STONE!*